WOMEN
+ Other Crimes

DAVID BODY

Alphonse Gaston Publishers

Women & Other Crimes

For information about this title or to order other books and/or electronic media, contact the publisher:
Alphonse Gaston Publishers
davidwbody1937@hotmail.com

ISBN: 979-8-9866948-0-1 (softcover)
        979-8-9866948-1-8 (eBook)

Edited by Susan T. Landry | susantlandry@gmail.com
Cover/Book Design | 1106Design.com

Dedicated to

Susan T. Landry

Editor, Mentor, Friend

Scratch a lover, and find a foe.

—Dorothy Parker, "Ballade of a Great Weariness"
in *Enough Rope*, 1926

Contents

CHAPTER I

THE ACCIDENT
A CLIFF-HANGER

Their car is skidding over black ice. It smashes through the railing and sails over the cliff. And it's over before he knows what hit him. Or rather her. She's the one who's shattered, crushed, and dead—still inside their car as it tumbles wildly down the ravine. He watches, prostrate on the pavement.

They're both a little drunk. She's driving. Fast over black ice. The car starts swerving, uncontrolled. He's jostled to his senses. The images that flash across his view from the front passenger seat are swirling around: streetlights, an 18-wheeler semi, a guardrail, a cliff edge. All in and out of focus. His only instinct is survival. He braces his left hand against her right shoulder. He flicks off his seat belt and pushes open his car door and rolls out onto the pavement without a second to spare, before their car soars over the precipice.

*　　*　　*

"I'll drive," he announced.

"I don't think so. You've had enough."

"And I'm fine."

"How many did she have, by the way?"

"Who's that?"

"That would be Harry's wife, the woman you spent the evening drinking with. She seems able to hold her liquor. I noticed only a slight lurch in her maneuvers around you. You, on the other hand, seemed to be swaying a bit. Losing your touch, dear?"

"Aren't you the little snoop. Why? Aren't we joined at the hip, my love?"

"We haven't been joined anywhere for years. In fact, I've been thinking we're so unjoined it hardly seems worth the effort."

"What are you saying?"

"What do you think I'm saying? It's called divorce. And I think it's about time."

"Wait, where did this come from? Let's try to work it out. We need each other, don't we?"

"I guess you need my money. But all good things, as they say."

"Please."

"Actually, I've been considering it for a while. And it's over. Believe me. Anyway, time to get out of here. Car's around here somewhere. But I can't seem to remember exactly where ..."

"We know how difficult this devastating tragedy must be for you. We just need to clear up a few loose ends."

"I've been over this with the other officers, more than once. It's difficult for me to keep it straight in my mind."

"I can well understand. And I'll keep our time together to a minimum. Now, you told the officers your wife skidded on a patch of black ice and swerved one way to avoid an approaching semi. Then she overreacted the other way, went through the guard railing, and over the cliff."

"Yes, that's what I remember. But it's really a bit hazy in my mind. My last memory is laying flat on the pavement and seeing our car plunging over the cliff. That image—I can't get it out of my mind."

"Of course. Now it seems she was wearing a seat belt but yours was unfastened."

"Guess I forgot to clip it. I'm sure you discovered from people at the party that we'd both had a few drinks."

"And your door was open. And you were thrown out."

"Yes. I guess so, as I've already stated. I remember I instinctively reached out and pushed against my wife, holding her back in a sort of protective move. It all happened so fast. I must have been pitched toward my door and flung out, but she ... I can't believe it."

"Well, you signed that prenup," said the lawyer, "which limits your inheritance. And she was in the process of cutting you off completely. She was going over a new will with me just before the accident. It's almost like you anticipated and took steps. But you couldn't have. Could you?"

"No. Of course not. I mean this all happened so fast. So just when did she review her will?"

"We talked last week."

"Last week? She said she wanted out but I never …"

"So you knew something was up?"

"I guess. But that bitch owed me something. Who else knows about her will rejigging?"

"Just me. Why?"

"Oh, no reason. Is it signed and notarized?"

"Not quite yet. Didn't get that far."

"Really, tell me more."

"She wanted a couple of last-minute changes. Some additional support guarantees for your son, including his full-time caregiver, in the assisted living home."

"I hate calling my son's home assisted living. That's so demeaning."

"Well, he'll always need support. A helping hand to live as normal a life as possible. What I mean is—"

"Never mind. I understand. What's normal to some isn't to others. By the way, who's in charge of our, that is my, son's care now?"

"That would be the trust."

"And just who calls the shots in the trust?"

"That's a little complicated, what with your wife gone so suddenly and all; but essentially, for now, that would be me."

"Really. Let's chat a little more about that trust. How much are we talking about here?"

"Certainly enough to take care of your son for the rest of his life."

"And who administers the 'enough' funds?"

"Presently, there are no specific provisions for the long-term administration of the trust. Your wife and I were due to meet and go over that detail."

"How about going over that detail now?"

"I'm not so sure this is a proper discussion for us."

"For who, then? He's my son and I would like to see he's taken care of."

"And he was her son. And she was in the process of writing you out of her will."

"Not quite a done deal, from what you say. And we're talking about a lot of money here. Just how much you would know better than I. And, of course, you also know the law better than I. But I'm thinking that if both of our names were, somehow, on that trust, and neither of us said anything about what might have been on a last-minute will change, well, we could both benefit—a lot. Everybody involved would benefit, including my son, of course. And everybody not involved would be none the wiser. Everybody's a winner. Right?"

"I could be disbarred for this kind of talk."

"You could be in for a windfall for this kind of talk."

"We've asked you to come to the police station because your son's full-time caregiver has requested we make further inquiries into the circumstances surrounding your wife's untimely death. Now, you should know your son's caregiver has hired a lawyer to help manage this investigation. Would you like to have your own lawyer present while we question you?"

"I don't see why that would be necessary. I thought everything was settled. My main concern here is my son. And I understood he's taken care of for the rest of his life. Which I'm very happy about."

"Yes. Papers signed and notarized. Her lawyer is listed as a trustee. You are listed as a parent overseer with discretionary powers over funds designated for your son's care. These funds are allocated by your deceased wife's attorney. The powers given to you in the will deal with legal matters I'm not qualified to address. Our concern now involves a few new details that have arisen around the accident. And understand, nobody is saying it was anything other than an unfortunate incident. But there is one circumstance that has come up concerning your wife and her situation in the car. It seems your wife was wearing a shiny, metallic silver dress. One that would easily hold fingerprints. Yours, to be precise."

"I don't understand. What's your point?"

"Now your recorded statement is that you reached over and pushed your wife back to protect her. But the evidence does not support that account. Your fingerprints are not on the front of your wife's dress. They are, in fact, on her shoulder. Indicating a forceful move away. Would you like to change your account? Would you like a lawyer? Realize, sir, there are no criminal charges here. We simply want to set the record straight. Any legal matters involving the will and estate are a separate issue."

"I only remember what I remember. And what comes to mind is that I did not, in any way, cause the accident or my wife's death. And I don't feel the need for a lawyer."

"I don't need my law degree to realize you used your wife as a support to shove yourself out of the car. While she ..."

"You weren't there, and you have no idea. So shut up about it. Just tell me where I stand in the will you prepared."

"Listen to me. You are not charged with homicide in your wife's death. But your actions during those moments of stress could serve as ammunition for a character assassination. Your character. If the details of that accident were to be made public, say, by your son's caregiver. As it stands presently, the legal papers I have released from this office give me the power to administer the funds in your deceased wife's trust. Funds to be used to benefit your son. Now, as the lawyer for your son's caregiver has discovered, I have liberal discretionary power in allocating those funds. Including the ability to channel funds through you. You're in the catbird seat. Money-wise."

"Then I guess it has all worked out for the best. Thank you very much."

"Before you go off half-cocked, you might want to consider the ramifications of releasing those accident details involving your actions around your wife in the car. What if you were ostracized and blacklisted in your social and professional friends' eyes? Not a pretty picture for a social animal."

"What's your point? My only concern is that will. Does it stand up? And fuck that caregiver. She can publish whatever."

"Fine. So I have gone to great lengths to protect my interests and also to set you up in a beneficial manner. Not to worry on my account. You, on the other hand, are vulnerable."

"Do I give a tinker's damn?"

"Your son's caregiver thinks the community will. And perhaps you should too."

"Perhaps I don't give a shit."

"I advise you to sit down with your son's caregiver. She wants to do it without lawyers. And I think you would do well to take her up on her offer."

"I only want justice for my son and myself."

"Now first of all, you should know I did not kill my wife. It was an accident. One I had nothing to do with."

"That very well may be true. But as your son's caregiver, I'm concerned about how his father's reputation reflects on my charge and his family's name. About how you acted during the accident. And what you're trying to do now."

"I'm trying to make sure my son is taken care of."

"You're trying to take care of yourself. Big time. And let me tell you that I will take care of you and your reputation as a sleazebag, if you don't go along with me."

"Just what do you want from me?"

"I want you to relinquish your hold on your deceased wife's funds."

"You want to cut me off completely?"

"Not completely. I'll furnish you with an allowance. Which is more than your wife was planning on."

"How much of an allowance?"

"That's my decision. It will probably vary. Depending on your attitude, your lifestyle, and just how much good I observe you doing for your son. For example, it's ten o'clock in the morning and you've been drinking. I would not want you to be doing any drinking around your son."

"Fuck you and your own attitude. You can do whatever you want with my reputation. I've got the money. And I'm going to keep it."

"Is that your final say on the matter?"

"You're goddamn right it is, pain in the ass."

"Fine. Now, I'm very late to meet your son and I could certainly use a ride back to his home."

"Okey dokey, if you're sure you don't mind riding along with a driver who's had a few."

* * *

"Well, one thing's for sure. You no longer need worry yourself over legal issues surrounding the actions of your charge's father after the unfortunate fatal accident. It would seem you are now responsible for the dispersion of funds allocated to their son by the family's lawyer. Funds from the inheritance of his mother's estate. How weird is it that his father just died in a car accident very much like the one his mother died in only a month ago. Similar circumstances. Similar location. Certainly is a strange happenstance, wouldn't you say? Anyway, would you like me to go with you to the police station, and continue on as your lawyer?"

"No, thank you. I'll be fine. I'm obliged to you for all your work. If I need you for any further advice, I'll call."

* * *

"Appreciate you coming down to the police station, miss. This shouldn't take long. But it's surely bizarre. Seems like only yesterday I was in this very room talking with your charge's father about his wife's fatal car accident. And now we're here talking about the father."

"Yes. How can I help you?"

"Well, the facts are a bit different here. The father seems to have simply driven his car off the cliff. Did he seem suicidal to you?"

"I really can't answer that question. I know he had been drinking. And I indicated to him I did not want him to see his son while in that condition. And that seemed to upset him. He was disturbed about a lot of things, actually. Including details surrounding the wife's accident."

"So, as to the particulars of the father's accident: You were in the passenger's seat?"

"Yes, I asked him to drive me to his son's home. He had been drinking and asked me if I minded riding with a driver who had a few. I said I was late. And had little choice in the matter."

"And he just drove off the cliff? What was your reaction?"

"Panic. He was driving like a madman. And when he started heading for the cliff, I, well, I just pushed myself out of the car. I didn't see any other choice."

"Now, his seat belt was fastened. Yours not. His car door open, your passenger side door closed. How did you get out?"

"The open window."

"Why not open the door?"

"The lock mechanism is confusing. I just squeezed myself out the window. I'm small."

"So you're familiar with the car?"

"Yes, I drive it often to transport his son. But the lock is still confusing."

"Okay, I'll drive you to my son's home. I suppose you'll want your own car now. Well, don't count on it."

"Hey, don't push me around like that. I know where my car is. It's the fucking keys I can't seem to find."

"Don't you worry about that," Caregiver said. "I've got my own set … and the car's right here. Now, you just slide in …

"Wait a minute, what the fuck are you doing?"

"I'm sitting on your lap while I drive this car. I drive it all the time transporting your son. And I can drive it with you right where you are."

"HEY … Get off me, you bitch!"

"You just hold still."

"What the hell are you doing? … Cut out this shit. You're driving like a madman."

"Madwoman. Now you just hold on tight."

"How fast are you going?"

"Fast enough."

✳   ✳   ✳

"One detail I still don't get in that fatal car accident police report. The one regarding that guy who just drove off the cliff, right before his son's caregiver jumped out."

"What is it?"

"The automatic speed control was set at full throttle. I asked her if she knew anything about that."

"What did she say?"

"She has no idea. He was driving like a madman. Said she just jumped out."

"Sounds like a good idea to me."

CHAPTER 2

OPEN AND SHUT

"Hi. Good weekend?"

"Same ole, same ole. Why the dickens you ask?"

"Hey, are you all right? Just being neighborly. Sorry man."

"Of course you're just being neighborly. What else? That's what neighbors are for. So they tell me. Got things on my mind is all."

"Understand. We both have. Say, I noticed your front door was open last night. I closed it. I thought you must have forgotten."

"You what? When was that?"

"Oh, I don't know. I got up to pee—you know how it is at our age—one or two o'clock, I guess."

"Holy cow! Was it wide open? Did you notice anything else? I mean, how did you even know it was open? Did you pee in the yard? Back up, man."

"Caught my eye out the bathroom window. I just stepped across and shut your door."

"You went clear across your backyard and around the fence. That's quite a hike. Were you in your shorts?"

"Well, yes, if you must know. And I tripped on something. But hey, sorry if it's a problem. Is it a problem? Are you actually mad?"

"No, no, of course not. Why should I be mad? Not at all."

"Good, because if I did something to get your goat, I'm sorry. You have another beer in that cooler?"

"Here, take it. Don't be a jerk. Not a problem. It's … well, nothing."

"Nothing what?"

"Truth is if I had seen your door open, I wouldn't have …"

"It was wide open! And what's so awful about it that you wouldn't do?"

"Touch it. You touched it. I wouldn't have touched somebody else's property."

"Right. But I'll say this much: You wouldn't see anything funny if you did come over and closed my door."

"What the hell do you mean by that?"

"Listen, I didn't go any farther than your top step. The door was wide open—enough for anyone to see inside, even if it was just for a second."

"And what do you claim you saw?"

"What do you think I saw? It was pitch black. Early morning. What could I have seen?"

"You're playing games with me. Did you see something or not?"

"This is weird. Because I thought I saw … but then … aw, let's forget the whole thing. I know nothing. I saw nothing. I closed nothing."

"Hey, you opened your big mouth. You opened the can of worms. Tell me whatever bullshit's on your mind."

"You're the bullshitter. I mean, I do you a favor and you're at me like … like I've done something terrible. Hurt you, violated you somehow. What's with that? You tell me."

"I'm saying I wouldn't have, is all. We're both loners. We agreed to stay that way. Have nothing to do with each other. Made a deal. Remember?"

"You might want to understand what I thought I saw. Pitch black or not. And this is me walking over, walking back. So out of the corner of my eye. Not looking for anything, mind you. And now I'm just kind of thinking back".

"Corner of your eye? Sounds like you were stalking me."

"You can take it any way you want, buddy. You want to know what I may have seen? Thought I saw. And heard, for that matter."

"Heard? What did you hear? You were stalking."

"Listen, we can drop this whole thing. Doesn't matter to me one way or the other. Not one iota. This beer hits the spot."

"There's plenty more."

"Thanks."

"Now tell me what the fuck you think you may have seen. Now we've gone this far."

"First of all, your wife's out of town. Right?"

"Of course, just like yours. We can agree on that. Your point?"

"I'm laying the groundwork. It's only you at home."

"I told you, she's at her sister's."

"And the house is empty?"

"I had friends over, for God's sake."

"At two in the morning?"

"Would you cut the crap and tell me what you think you saw? And we can put this whole business to rest."

"Fine. Well it was dark, very dark, as I've already said. But I'm pretty sure I spotted two figures by the door. Didn't see any faces. I'm guessing both male."

"So now you're guessing. At what you think you saw. Or didn't."

"Right. But then I'm walking away and I could have sworn I heard a click, like the sound when I eased your door shut because I didn't want to wake anybody. And I was curious and I looked around."

"Don't tell me. More guessing."

"OK, OK, everything was dark, inside and out. But maybe, just maybe I saw a black smudge of a guy carrying what might have been a large object, a package, maybe a suitcase, but he seemed to be lugging it over his shoulder. Sort of zigzaggy, like it's heavy. It's dark, everything's blurry and all. Middle of the night, and I'm groggy … still.

Oh yeah; and something else to muddy the water. I think Mary—you know that old hag next door who spends her life spying—saw me. Her light went on after I tripped and made a sound. Just saying."

"So what? Mary Schmary. Bullshit. Total bullshit. You didn't see a thing."

∗   ∗   ∗

"So, you've already stated your wife told you she was going to her sister's in Raymond."

"Three days ago, Officer. She was going to help with the kids. She's not there, and I haven't heard from her. But, like I said, this isn't the first time. We've been over all this, more than once."

"I know, I know. We're only looking at some details. One of your neighbors said he closed your door and another neighbor said she spotted someone in the yard—let me check my notes—this was the night of the same day your wife left."

"Yeah, I heard about the neighbors. Did they see anything? Sounds like fake news to me."

"Nothing definite. Too dark."

"Fine. Am I through here?"

"Yes. You are. Now, you said you don't want a lawyer. Still feel that way?"

"Yes. Why? Are you accusing me of something? Are you saying I need one? Because to me, guys with lawyers are guilty. Isn't that what you think? And I'm innocent. Of whatever."

"Not at all. We respect your decision. Oh, and one last thing. Your neighbor's wife also seems to be missing. Know anything about that?"

"Know anything? What the heck would I know? I hardly knew the woman. Yeah, we were neighbors, but aside from an occasional backyard get-together, couple of beers, burgers, you know, we really didn't see much of each other."

"Both with same names."

"Yeah, Sophie and Sophie. They were the ones who talked to each other, really. But you must know that."

"We do."

"Right, we did joke about it. The same name. What are the odds of that? Neighbors and all. Kind of like how we met. Weird, isn't it?"

"It is."

"So, look. Am I all done here?"

"For now. Please stay in town. We'll be in touch with any further questions."

✶　✶　✶

"Now, you've already told us that your Sophie—do you mind if I refer to her as your Sophie? The same name thing and all?"

"Why should I mind, for God's sake? Doesn't matter to me."

"We know, only asking. So, your neighbor's wife went to her sister's, according to your neighbor."

"You have any reason to not believe him?"

"We don't know who to believe, sir. This is a police investigation into missing persons. If they're missing."

"If they're missing? They're not here. I'd say they're missing. You've already asked me I don't know how many questions. Perhaps it's time to start looking."

"Yes, sir. Now it does seem a bit unusual that both your wives go missing at the same time. You said your wife said nothing to you? Could they have gone off together?"

"As I've already said, I don't think so. What did my neighbor say?"

"Same thing. We're double-checking is all. By the way, as part of this investigation, mind you, I must ask you how you and your wife were getting along."

"What kind of a goddamn question is that? We were getting along just fine. Sure, we had our ups and downs, like any couple. But I miss her. And I want you to find her."

*　　*　　*

"Well, there you go. Sophie Two's husband's same answer as Sophie One's: ups and downs, both miss them. Almost the same words. Making anything of it?"

"Not that would lead to anything productive for now. But I'm going to stay on the case."

POLICE BLOTTER
SAME NAME WIVES VANISH ON SAME DAY.
Husbands mystified, distraught.

✳ ✳ ✳

"So, do you guys have any objection to us continuing to call your wives Sophie One and Sophie Two?"

"Hey. Where did you come from?"

"How did we find you two in this tropical paradise? We can usually find people who are still alive. The real problem was connecting you guys to the remains of the two Sophies we found. You see, it was the series of events that got us to thinking. As you told us, you went over and closed your neighbor's door. Pitch dark. Tripped and made a sound on the way. Got another neighbor's attention—I think you were kind enough to call her a 'nosy old bag.' And she looked over and saw someone leave the house. Kept looking, and nobody returned. Said the guy who left was carrying something. Something pretty big. We did a search of the area your nosy neighbor pointed out. Found some fabric scraps. But that didn't give us enough to go on until we found the remains of Sophie One. DNA led us to a known lowlife, who sang like the former jailbird he is. We made him an offer he couldn't refuse, and he finally said all he did was get rid of two bags. Had no idea what was in them. Showed us where the other one was. Fabric scraps matched those near your place.

"Your mistake? Oh, I don't know. Hiring one guy to do two jobs. Not double-checking on what a scumbag that guy was. Tripping and attracting your neighbor's attention … killing your wives in the first place. The list goes on. And oh yeah, it would have helped if the guy you hired had closed the door on his way out."

CHAPTER 3

A Few Things That Happened Before Bunny Croaked

"Hello, we've never met, but here's the thing: My wife, Bunny, gave me this cell phone number last week, just before she passed away, actually—right, well thank you—but she lived a good long life, natural causes. A few years older than me. Now, next to this number is a name, nickname I guess: 'Life Saver.' Are you Life Saver?"

"Yeah, that's what Bunny tagged me with last I saw her."

"So you must have been real good friends with my wife."

"Knew each other from way back."

"Right, and she said I could call this number if I wanted to learn something about her past."

"Call this number if you wanted to learn something about her past? Hmmm …"

"Yes. You see, we met later in life. And our agreement was to not question each other in too much detail about our backgrounds. She said she wasn't real proud of some things in her past. Wanted a fresh start. I was fine with that. I assume you were one of her past lovers?"

"No, I wasn't. It's a bit messy. But we did keep in touch. Quick checks now and then, just to see how things were going. Said she married a cop, said he was a real nice guy. That's all I know about you. Mentioned two kids. No details. We hadn't talked in more than, oh, five years. Knew she was ill. Sorry she croaked. I liked her. Smart. Don't even know how you guys met."

"I was introduced to Bunny during a routine police interrogation. We found her name in a mobster's address book. Called her into the station just to check her out. Nothing ever came of it. But something happened that's really not supposed to happen. We were attracted to each other, and well, eventually, we got married."

"Okay, so you called. We talked. Thanks for giving me the dope on Bunny's end. We done here?"

"No, wait. What about what Bunny said you could tell me?"

"That would be?"

"You know very well. Background stuff."

"Right. You sure?"

"I'm sure."

"I'll give you my address. Live alone. Makes it easier to blab stuff. Tomorrow night, six."

———

"Come on in, get comfortable. Help yourself to a beer in the fridge. We can get started … if you're still sure you want the scoop."

"I want the scoop."

"Suit yourself. First, let me say again: I am not an old Bunny lover."

"That's good."

"If you say so. Wait till you hear the inside dope. Now let's see, guess I'll start at a Walmart."

"You two met at a Walmart?"

"I didn't meet Bunny at a Walmart. I didn't even know her then. I met my employer, at the time, at a Walmart. And he was late for the appointment he set up. And an asshole about it. As usual."

"Oh, there you are. I was looking for you," my employer said. "Where've you been?"

"Where've I been? Freezing my ass off, right here," I said, "where you told me to wait, boss, under this Walmart sign."

"You're paid to follow orders. Not to bitch. Now we need to get some garbage bags and duct tape."

"Fine. We'll get 'em tomorrow."

"Need them now. Store's closed. That sign look like it's got a light? Shit, I got held up. We've got to break in. Need the stuff now."

"You're crazy. Sorry, but why not tomorrow?"

"You listening? Look for a window, anything I can smash." So I bust in, grab some bags and tape. The alarm started screaming, wouldn't you know. Got out just in time. Could have been nabbed for sure. All because he doesn't pay no attention to time or nothing or no one. Especially to me."

"Good. That's done," my employer said. "Now we need to do some wrapping and taping. Stuff's in my trunk. Here's the key. Open it up."

"Now, he wants me to open his trunk, or sombody's trunk, in somebody's big-ass mobster limo. The one he's driving. That's my employer, a made guy, a contract killer, who does bad things to people, and puts 'em in trunks. Wants me to open this trunk. I'm thinking, I need a different kind of job.

"Why me?" I said. "You open it."

"What?" says my employer—the big, tough Contract Killer. "You scared of something you might find? Ha, ha."

"I know what I've found in other trunks of yours. And I don't really want to …"

"What are you afraid of? Open the trunk. And do it now."

"Okay, if you say so."

"I say so …"

"Hey, it's just clothes," I said. "What's this all about?"

"Don't you worry," Contract Killer said. "Just stuff them in those bags and tape them up."

"Looks like a guy's uniform and a doorman or chauffeur hat. And I'm looking at a ritzy blouse and skirt from some high-class bitch. What it looks like to me."

"I don't give a shit what it looks like to you. Just shove everything in. Actually, guy's gear in one bag, girl's in another. Seal them up and stick them in the trunk."

"Good. That business is taken care of," Contract Killer said. "Now we're going to stash this limo with the clothes. And wait."

"Wait for what?"

"You don't have to worry about that. But then, I might as well fill you in on a few details. First, we hide the car. And it's your job to stay close. Keep an eye on it. Needs to stay safe and sound. I just wait for a call. You sit tight till you hear from me. Then we take the clothes and show them to somebody. After that business is taken care of, we chuck the clothes."

"I don't get it."

"You don't need to get anything. Just follow orders. I'll call."

But in short order, I had to call with some bad news …

"Hey, didn't I say for you to wait for my call? Don't call me," said Contract Killer. "What do you want?"

"See the paper?" I said.

"Don't read the paper."

"Me neither, usually. But my girlfriend does the cross-words. She's always coming up with words I never heard of, like pip. Do you know pip is a bird sickness? And it's also—"

"What are you talking about? I told you not to call me and now you call talking about some kind of bird shit. Shut up, hang up, and don't—"

"No, wait. What I'm really calling about is the news in the paper, not the crosswords that my girlfriend is always—"

"I don't give a shit about your girlfriend … what news?"

"News about a body found in Casco Bay. A guy. Nude. Big reward if anybody knows anything."

"What? I'm sure there's a big reward. Big reward for you if you say anything to anybody."

"I'm not saying anything. I'm just saying …"

"So don't."

"I know. But shouldn't we get rid of the clothes? I mean, there could be a connection and we could be in trouble."

"You think so? Nothing gets by you. Just stay scarce. Should hear something soon."

Then he called me and I had to give him the news. That's when the shit really hit the fan.

"Okay, glad you answered your phone so soon," said Contract Killer. "Paying attention for a change. Time to move. Got a place to take the stuff. We meet this guy. Lay out the clothes we stashed in the trunk. Just the girl stuff, actually. But I'll fill you in on everything when I see you at the place where we squirreled away the car."

"Listen," I said. "I've got some news."

"What? Give it to me later."

"Car ain't there."

"What the fuck are you talking about?"

"Hear me out, please. Went for a ride."

"No."

"Can't help it. See, I go for a ride. Keys are in the car where you left them and I thought—"

"Thought what, asshole?"

"Let me tell you the whole story. Important."

"No shit."

"So, I goes for a quick joy ride. Got bored. Didn't see no harm."

"I don't believe this."

"I remember where you left the keys. In back, under the mat. Don't remember left or right. Looked at both. At first I think right. But turns out it's—"

"Shut up with the stupid stuff and just—"

"I roll along after I visit a liquor store. Not fast 'cause don't want to get stopped or nothing. But then this cop starts following me with his blue flasher lights on. And I think, oh shit. What if he looks in the trunk and … what if? Anyway, I speed up. And then I think that's not going to work. Read about chases and cops always get the car. See I read the paper, like I told you, my girlfriend does the crosswords, and that's how …"

"Get on with it."

"So I stop. And I sees this cop walking up to the car, real slow like. I get out and that's when I notice my blinker lights are on. Blinkers on the whole time. Double blinkers! I used the double kind cause I couldn't find a parking place at the liquor store, so I just parked on the road and put the blinkers on, 'cause I don't want to get hit, and I must have left them on the whole time. Ain't that a riot?"

"Please tell me this story isn't true."

"I ain't finished yet. I run, and the cop, well, he runs after me. So I run behind a house, or apartment, can't remember—"

"Just tell me what happened."

"What happened? I'm running, over a fence, behind a tree, over a bush, and I look behind, and he's still there. I can't believe it. But I keep running and finally, when I look, he's gone. Yeah, gone! Didn't I do good?"

"You did shitty. Real shitty. The car's gone. With the clothes. And I'm fucked."

"I know, I know. I didn't show," Contract Killer said to his mafia boss client. "And you said not to call. But please listen. Job's done: I did that rat-fink chauffeur of that other mafia boss, Boss Duo, 'cause you're Boss Uno, right?"

"Just get on with it."

"Right. And I did your two-timing girlfriend. What you asked for. Don't need me to show you anything. His and her clothes are in the trunk of the car the cops stopped. And they found the chauffeur, dead in the river. So both are taken care of. Did what you said. How do you want to pay me?"

"Pay you for what?" said Boss Uno. "You're not finished with the job."

"What's the problem?"

"I don't like it. Don't like any of it. First of all, where is she?"

"Look, you got her clothes."

"Yeah, you say they're in the trunk of the car at the police station. What's with that? I certainly can't wander into the station, all casual like, and have a look in the trunk. Deal was for them to disappear and for you to show me their clothes, both, as proof. So you didn't live up to your part."

"My guy fucked up. My problem. But you know the job's done. Don't you?"

"I know they found so-called fucking Duo Boss's dead chauffeur. Done deal. But even that's not so great because I think we said both should vanish. Him and her. Didn't we say that?"

"Yeah, well, shit happens, can't always figure out the tide and current stuff. But you got what you wanted."

"What I wanted was for two to be dead, my cheater girlfriend and her chauffeur lover. Both to leave the scene. So he shows up. Why wasn't she with him?"

"Don't know. Like I said, can't figure everything. You got him. Her clothes are in the car at the police station."

"That's what you say. But I need to be sure. Something just doesn't feel right here. Let's meet after I do some checking. And then you can answer a few questions. Better answer them real good."

"He's not completely sold," Contract Killer said to Bunny. "Thanks to my fuck-up, asshole helper guy. Got to convince Boss Uno you're dead. Hope I don't have to kill you for real."

"Very fucking funny," she said. "We've got a deal. How about you killing him? Or fix it so I can kill him. That I would like."

"I'm sure. Then both your former lovers would be gone. Boss Uno as well as Boss Duo's chauffeur. You really know how to pick 'em."

———

You see, it happened like this: Contract Killer didn't kill her along with him, like he was supposed to for Boss Uno. 'Cause, at the very last minute, I mean just after he bumps off Chauffeur Lover and turns the gun on her, she jumps up faster than a speeding bullet, so to speak, with this crazy, wild-ass promise. See, she's not only gorgeous, she's smart. That would be your wife. She swore to share something valuable with this guy. She says it's a book of incriminating names and addresses that Chauffeur Lover stole from Boss Duo while working for him. Says she and her Chauffeur were just about to sell it to her other lover, Boss Uno. That's before Boss Uno finds out what's going on. So Boss Uno hires Contract Killer to take care of both of 'em. But she's something else. "Fake my death," she purrs, "I got the book. We can sell it. Contains names and addresses worth a lot to Boss Uno, believe me. You decide. But you need me in order to get that book. Kill me and you've lost something worth its weight in gold." That's what she tells Contract Killer to save her ass. That's her story. And he falls for it. So now Contract Killer's got to convince Boss Uno that the whole job's done. And then find a way to sell Boss Uno this prized book of names and addresses belonging to Boss Duo.

———

"Okay, let's straighten this whole thing out," says Contract Killer to Boss Uno. "You know the job's done. What more can I say?"

"Not so fast, buddy," says Boss Uno.

"What?"

"I got a friend at the station. And you're right. He says all her clothes are in the trunk, along with Chauffeur Lover's clothes. And a wedding ring."

"Yeah. The ring. I saw it."

"Well, it's her mother's wedding ring. I had it remounted. I know it's very sentimental to her. Actually two rings. A regular ring and this clip-on part. She would not want to lose that ring. So anyway, my cop friend says: 'Here, you take it.' And he gives me the ring. Says they don't need it for their investigation. So listen up, the part he gives me is the clip-on thing. Not the main ring. Somebody must of separated them. Figured one part is enough. Nobody else would notice it's the clip-on, not the real ring. So let's say somebody wanted to leave a clip-on part as evidence of a job done. And then keep the genuine ring 'cause it's more important. It's a sentimental thing. See, she could take one and leave one. With no one the wiser. But I'm the wiser, aren't I? 'Cause she's alive, isn't she?"

"No, wait. I can explain."

"You can tell me where she is and I just might let you live. If you don't, you're dead. You're dicking her, aren't you? First Boss Duo's Chauffeur Lover does my girlfriend and then they both start dealing. And now you? She's something else."

"No, please, I'm not dicking her, believe me. I just met her doing your job. Will you give me a break?"

"You lead me to her and I just might go easy on you. You did half the job. Sort of. Anyway, you have no choice."

"We're in trouble, Bunny," Contract Killer said. "We need to get out of here. Sorry to put you in this underground garage, but I need you in a safe place while I work things out … I'll be back."

"Car's ready, boss," I said to Contract Killer.

"Are you sure nobody followed you?"

"I drove all over. Even went through that cemetery on the east end. The one with the duck pond. You know the one I'm talking about?"

"Please stop talking. Let's go."

"Actually, only two of us are going. Me and your girl partner."

"You shut the fuck up and show us where the car is."

"Matter of fact, there are two cars, make that limos, out there. One for you, and one for me and your girl partner, plus two mafia bosses—bosses who made a peace deal. Come to terms. Thanks in part to your girl partner. You see, she's worked both sides of the fence. And we convinced both mafia guys that two people stood in the way of a settlement. First, the rat-fink Cheater Chauffeur of Boss Duo, who wanted to play one side against the other, and who was no good to either side. Then there's you, who tried to pull a fast one. Not being straight with finishing off a job for Boss Uno. A big no-no to any mafia boss."

"Wait a minute, what about her? She's part of this deal. Is she free and clear?"

"Good question. But you see, after some haggling, they both finally decided she was just an order taker. Caught in the middle of a ugly situation."

"I don't understand. How did you get involved?"

"Another good question. I pay attention. Talk to people. Saw you two were up to something. And it seemed to me no good could come of whatever you and your girl partner were setting up. So I moved in quickly. Went to her. Nothing to lose. We sorted things out. And we took a chance and went to both sides with a kind of a compromise, one without any address book and ransom payment garbage. They were surprised at first. But then said it made sense. And a deal was worked out for them to come to terms. A deal minus Chauffeur and you. Chauffeur's gone. But you're still around. Sorry ..."

"I must say, feels good for our gangs not to be constantly doing battle with each other," the boss said.

"Yeah, two gangs working together are better that two working apart. Without all those incriminating names and addresses held over our heads for bullshit ransom payments. Wouldn't you say?"

"I would say."

"Thanks to the scheming of those two in the back seat: Bunny and her business partner. Pretty smart wheeler-dealers."

"Don't suppose you two would both like jobs? Good pay and benefits."

"Thanks, but no thanks."

"Didn't think so. So where can we take you?"

"We've agreed to go our separate ways, thank you. Right here is fine for me. And I think that bus stop around the next corner would be good for Bunny."

"Yeah. It's been real. Bye … And you know something? I think I'll call you Life Saver."

———

"So, you sorry you heard our story?"

"We had a good life together. She turned over a new leaf. What about you?"

"Once a freelancer, always a freelancer."

CHAPTER 4

A Naughty Tattoo Comes Out of the Closet

"You're late, as usual. What the heck do you do in the bathroom that takes you so long? Us women are supposed to dawdle in the powder room. Not you men."

"I don't know about male/female differences in the powder room. I just take care of my business. Time to go."

"Fine. I'll drive. But you've got to help me with the directions. I can never remember left or right at that red barn."

"Left. And it's blue."

———

"Whatever; let's get a move on."

———

"Now why in the world," grumbled Sarah, "do you suppose these two live so far away, in the damn boonies for God's sake. I mean an hour-and-a-half drive for dinner seems a bit much. Yeah, I know she's easy to get along with and all, but he always makes such a big fuss about silly little things, like two remarkable kinds of wine, and that stupid amuse-bouche thing. Then there's always a new, fancy-dancy dish he wants to try out. Frankly, I'm really fed up with his whole foodie scene. I would just as soon call off our regular dinner get-togethers."

"Hey, wait a minute here, Sarah. What's your problem? Don't you like the dinners? We're all friends, aren't we? I mean, how many years has it been?"

"Ages. You two always seem to be having a grand time with the guy talk and all. But seems like Mary Ann and I run out of things to chat about before the main course even arrives. The same main course he spends oodles of time bragging about and fishing around for compliments. Isn't it enough that you two go off every weekend or so to have fun together? What do you guys talk about besides golf, anyway?"

"Stuff. You know. Sometimes his Civil War gun collection. Whatever."

"That Civil War arsenal scares me. Do any of his guns actually work?"

"Maybe. Not really sure. Some do, I guess. You have something against the Civil War?"

"No, I don't know. But that's fine. Only the dinners are getting to be tedious."

"He loves preparing dinners for us. And he thinks we enjoy them. I know I do."

"Yeah, well while you two are having such a grand time, we're a sideshow. Spending our time watching you guys laughing and giggling."

"Giggling? Do we giggle? We're just shooting the breeze about things."

"Well, let me tell you something. You two are giggling. Just like a couple of …"

"Of what?"

"Of, well, like a couple of old women. There I said it. And that's what it looks like. We talk about it every now and then."

"Talk. How?"

"Talk. You know, talk about how you guys appear."

"How do we appear? What are you saying?"

"I'm not saying anything. I'm just saying that … Look, can't we have a conversation about something else?"

"Fine. You first."

"Okay, what do you suppose tonight's amuse-bouche will be? It's a surprise. I'm not supposed to say anything to you."

"Oh? Just when did you talk to him about a surprise?"

"When? I don't remember," said Sarah. "Must have been a few days ago. I don't know."

"Was it when you spent half the night on the computer?"

"No, no, that was a business thing."

"Really? Well, more and more business things seem to be coming up lately. Are you sure everything's all right?"

"Everything's fine. I am curious about one thing he let slip awhile ago. It was concerning a tattoo. Like he's got one but he won't say where."

"It's personal."

"What?"

"Personal, I think. I'm not really sure."

"When did you learn about a tattoo of his that's personal?"

"Oh, I don't know. I think I might heard him say something about it being in a private place. But I really can't recall."

"Well, that is so strange. I mean, I've asked him more than once. He brought it up. Maybe by accident. But then he clams up about where it is. And I asked Mary Ann and she insists she doesn't know anything. How could that be? But he told you it was in a personal place. Doesn't that seem weird to you?"

"I don't know. What's the difference? Why are you so obsessed with a tattoo?"

"I'm not obsessed. But this business just doesn't sit right. And that's a fact. Well, I'm going to ask him tonight."

"Ask him what?"

"What do you think? Ask him where his tattoo is."

"Don't."

"What do you mean, don't? It'll give me something to talk about besides his fancy-pants cooking."

"He's sensitive about that tattoo."

"What are you talking about? And how the dickens do you know he's so sensitive about a stupid tattoo?"

"I don't know. Can we just get off this subject?"

"I don't think so. I'd like to straighten out this whole tattoo business. Tell me what you know about it or I'll simply ask Mr. Sensitive when we finally arrive at his gourmet abode."

"Please."

"Please what? Please don't talk to you about it? Please don't talk to him about it? Please shut up? Well, we can. We can both shut up about it now. Because I'm going to start asking questions the minute we arrive. So there."

"I'm begging you."

"Okay. It's only that I'm a little curious. And I'm thinking that during a lull in this evening's foodie talk, I'll simply ask your near and dear friend about that tattoo."

"What do you mean by near and dear?"

"Nothing. Nothing at all. And you're off the deep end for some reason. Can you tell me why?"

———

"Well, I'm not one to brag. But I'll just say I believe you're all in for quite a surprise tonight. It's a recipe that just popped up in this Hungarian cookbook, one I found buried in my own gourmet library. It calls for a certain spice that I had a dickens of a time tracking down …"

"I see, would that be anything like a savory search?"

"Oh Sarah, you have such a marvelous sense of humor. Anyway, understand it's my first time with this particular bill of fare, so we can only hope for the best. Now, if you girls want to set the places and chitchat a bit, we'll just head on into the kitchen and get a few things in order for Hungarian gourmet."

———

"Careful with these plates, Mary Ann: Hungarian gourmet is on its way."

"Isn't that an oxymoron, Sarah?"

"Oh, I've had some reasonable Hungarian stew, accompanied by a shitload of hot sauce and globs of ketchup."

"If I had to choose between Hungarian fare and American mac and cheese, it would not be easy."

———

"It certainly smells scrumptious simmering on the stove, but I'm not going to quiz you on contents until I've had a taste."

"No, don't. But I'm betting you'll never name all that went into this, oh, I'll call it a creation. If I may."

"I'll be the judge of that and I can hardly wait."

"I'm so looking forward to your initial reaction."

"First, with your permission, I'll just go out and get the girls started with your amuse-bouche. Oh, by the way, let's not forget about our golf holiday. It's coming right up, you know."

———

"Why the fuck did you tell her your tattoo was on the back side of your Johnson? Why, why, why?"

"Because your scatterbrained wife wouldn't shut up her nonstop yap—that's why."

"So?"

"So … you were there! I finally caved and just told her where the stupid thing was."

"Yeah, and then I, like a damn fool, blurted out I knew where it was all along … that it was a pair of lips. That's when Mary Ann went crazy. After all these years, she finally discovered I knew more about your intimate yearnings than she did. That I was well aware of a small tattoo on the back side of your dick, something only visible to someone who, well, saw things back there. Things that apparently she didn't see because she didn't do certain stuff. And therefore we were … you know."

"I do. And tattoo or no, I'm kind of surprised that neither one of our wives ever caught on. I mean, after all these years?"

"I guess I am too."

"Well, Mary Ann, at long last, made the discovery. But why did she have to get so deranged?"

"More importantly, why did you have to respond like such a lunatic? Answer me that."

"You saw her, what else could I do?"

"What else? You could have just walked out of the room instead of grabbing that stupid Civil War Blunder Buster. Or whatever the hell it is. And gone berserk smashing her head with it."

"I lost it. She was out of control, crazed. You saw her."

"I did. Do you think your initial whack did her in?"

"I don't know. But she was a mess. And I felt I had no option but to bring it to an end with a mercy killing."

"I guess you were right."

"So, I owe you. Assume you felt you had no option but to go after Sarah? My only witness, other than you."

"Did I have a choice? Lucky you gave me a few lessons on how to actually shoot one of your gun collection relics."

"Tell me. What went through your mind?"

"Nothing really. I suppose I instinctively sized up the problem. Grabbed one of the guns and used it. She didn't even see me make a move. It was over before it even crossed my mind what I had done. So, what's the plan for Sarah and Mary Ann back there in your trunk?"

"There's a Civil War cemetery about two hours from here. It has a partially hidden, unknown-soldier mausoleum. I think that would be appropriate."

"Yes."

"Only one problem."

"Oh?"

"What the hell are we going to tell the police when they ask us what we know about the mysterious disappearance of our two lovely wives, while we were off on a golfing holiday?"

"Do you think they would buy this: They were having a secret love affair and ran off together?"

CHAPTER 5

A Bar Called Lucky's

etting dark unbearably early on these fall days… it's so depressing, he thought. *Only seven o'clock and I can hardly see my nose in front of my face. Plus, I'm freezing my ass off in this Siberian downpour. Add to all this, yet another crappy day at the office. I need a drink. Well … what do we have here? Appears to be a shabby sign for Lucky's Good-Time Bar & Grill. Looks good enough for me … Hold it … If Lucky would just fix his door so a person could open it without a crowbar … Okay, I got it … Feels good to just get in out of the rain … Dark as hell in here though … Wait a minute. Did I get that sign right? I mean, what is this? Since when does a bar have apartment buzzers? Shit. This can't be Lucky's. I'm out of here. Not sure Lucky's is worth it … Damn it to hell, the door I just opened is locked from the inside. Wait a minute, this other door to the apartments is secure. Looks like I need a buzzer reply to get into the apartments for some help. Can't get out, can't get in for Christ's sake. I'll try pushing one of these stupid buzzers …*

"Yeah? Who is it?" he answered.

"Oh, hi there. Look here, you don't know me. But I'm stuck in your entrance. I was looking for a drink, but then I—"

"What's that? Speak up. The intercom's for shit."

"You see, I was going to check out Lucky's, to get a quick one, but the sign wasn't what I thought. Appears I pushed your outside door by mistake, but it was jammed. I finally forced it open and got in. Now I can't get out. Well, here I am. Can you help me? I mean, what do I have to do to get out of here?"

"Who did you say you were you looking for?"

"Nobody. I'm sorry to disturb you. But I'm trapped down here and I just need for you to open the outside door, or buzz me up and loan me a key to get out, or something. Whatever it takes."

"I can't hear you. Just tell me who you want."

"I don't want anybody. I want out of here."

"You're not making any sense. But I'll take a wild-ass chance and buzz you up. And you can tell me just who the hell you're looking for. Second floor, first door on the left."

———

"Hi there. Listen, sorry about this. But the whole thing is so silly, you see. I'm not looking for anyone. I mean, I was trying to find Lucky's but the sign wasn't what I thought. Anyway, I seem to have gotten stuck in your lobby and I was just ..."

"Gotcha. Not the first one to be confused by Lucky's useless sign. You look like a decent person, but soaked. Want to dry off a bit before you face the elements?"

"I don't want to bother you, but ... that would be nice."

"Okey dokey, so step in. Here, let me get the crap off this chair so you can take a load off."

"No need. I'll stand. Not a problem."

"Sit! I know this place is kind of a mess. But it is what it is, I Yam What I Yam, as Popeye the Sailor Man says."

"Yes, I know about Popeye."

"Good, then we have something in common. Probably the only thing though."

"You think so?"

"Well, you've got a clean-shaven, Ivy League look, Brooks Brothers Guy, if I'm not mistaken. And I've got a beard been meaning to trim for months, plus I'm wearing an outfit could use a trip to the laundromat."

"You're fine. Going for the Ginsberg Wannabe look, I assume."

"I'm going for the Ginsberg talent. With no luck."

"You a writer?"

"Well, that all depends on your definition. Do I have to be published to be considered literary?"

"No."

"Then I'm a writer. Aspiring to be published. And you?"

"I write ads."

"Oh yeah? Like on TV?"

"TV, newspapers, magazines, matchbook covers. You name it."

"Really. Isn't that interesting? You like it? I mean, do you enjoy your work?"

"It's a paycheck. But I wouldn't exactly call it enjoyable."

"No? How come?"

"You take today. I went into my creative director's office I don't know how many times with I don't know how many different TV commercials, all for the same stupid-ass bank. All rejected. Tomorrow? Start all over with the same ole bullshit. Boy, the crap you have to take for a paycheck."

"So, your brilliant commercials get rejected, just like my literary masterpieces."

"Life sucks, doesn't it? Anyway, I gotta get going. Girlfriend'll be pissed if I'm late for dinner. Speaking of the crap a person has to take."

"Wait, horse pucky at the office, horse pucky on the home front. Now, perhaps I'm no one to talk about disappointing lifestyles, but you're no better off than I am. And now you're going to run home like a little puppy dog."

"Fuck you. What do you know? This place is a dump. Where do you get off telling me what's wrong with my life?"

"Sorry. You're right. My apologies for being such a rude asshole. But, off the top of my head, I'd say we could both use bit of a makeover. Now, here's a stupid thought: Call the girlfriend. Tell her you've been held up at the office. Can't make it home for dinner. Have dinner with me, here. We could fess up with each other about what's going on in our lives. Our thoughts. For better or for worse. Maybe it's a lame-brained idea. And we'll just go off on our merry ways. Be done with it. On the other hand, who knows? For example, I'll confess something. Because fact of the matter is, I'm obsessed with the Russian novel *Crime and Punishment*. I keep reading it. Over and over again. About how this guy kills because, well, just because. I'm intrigued with the idea. Now is that bad?"

"I don't know. I don't think so. And your notion about sticking around and discussing our own life situations is tempting and all, but I've got to go."

"Why?"

"Why? Because dinner's on the table. And she's … well, she likes to keep to her schedule."

"What about your schedule?"

"My schedule? I don't have one."

"That's good. Call her."

"Just told you. I can't."

"Yes you can."

"Can't."

"Can, asshole."

"This is so stupid. You're the asshole … Oh fuck it, I'll call her."

"Good for you. So you're not such an asshole after all. Dinner's pizza. I'll order. Can you chip in something?"

"I'll take care of it. Make mine anything vegetarian."

"You don't like meat?"

"Girlfriend's a vegan. So I just go along with whatever."

"I understand. Two large with pepperoni coming up. Listen, mind if I make it three guests? Girl down the hall and I are a sometime thing."

"Fine, make it three."

"Good. I'll invite her and take care of the pizza delivery. You can place your call, and if I can just borrow your credit card for a sec."

"So, how'd you guys connect? I mean, somehow I don't see you two together."

"It's a long story. We just met. He tagged me with the moniker Brooks Brothers Guy, I call him Ginsberg Wannabe. See, I was headed for Lucky's but ended up buzzing your boyfriend's apartment, and, well, we decided to have dinner, and then he mentioned you. And so here we are."

"We are. You got a girlfriend?"

"Yes. And aren't you the forward one."

"Oh, don't get me wrong. I'm not coming on to you. It's just that I'm an artist, and I'm interested in people's backgrounds. And you're a bit, oh I don't know … different from my writer friend here."

"Aren't you his girlfriend?"

"Now you're the forward one. And no. We get together every now and then."

"Hey! Pizza's here. You two hooking up? Is somebody gonna get painted? Or are we going have something to eat?"

"We're not hooking up. And I'm certainly not going to paint him."

"Why not? I'm not pretty enough for you?"

"You're too pretty. Too buttoned down. Too clean-cut. I like to paint guys and girls with character, people with flaws. Now, if you've got something off the wall about you, like, oh I don't know, a bendy penis, or three balls, then maybe … Just kidding."

"Oh, did I mention my neighbor friend is rude?"

"What's wrong with being rude? I am glad to see you're branching out and mingling with guys with regular, refined, day jobs. Are you tempted to join him?"

"I'm an equal-opportunity socializer. And it's enticing, but I'm not sure I see myself as a day-job kind of guy. We just met. He's good-natured enough. And it's weird, but we have certain things in common."

"What the hell are you talking about? You guys are night and day."

"You think so? I'll have you know our plan for tonight is to compare lives. Seems like we both could use a bit of a readjustment. Isn't that what we were talking about, my friend?"

"Readjustment? Well, that's not exactly what I had in mind."

"That is so funny. And I just had an even funnier idea. What if I painted both of you guys together? Each wearing your regular, goofy, polar-opposite outfits. And I could work on getting you two to show your own mismatched, lifestyle expressions."

"Well, it's been fun. But I think this party's over."

"Wait, my painting could turn out to be a masterpiece. I might even pay you. Even though I am a bit strapped just now. How about a blow job? Only kidding. But I'm thinking I really would like to paint you two."

"Blow job? For both of us?"

"Shut up, you pig of a hall mate."

"Listen, I think I should go."

"Okay. But will you even consider posing for me?"

"I'll consider it. Still, I gotta go."

"Hi there, my friend. Back again looking for Lucky's?"

"I can't believe I'm here in your apartment again. But I just got off work and I'd like a word with your hall mate. She around?"

"She's in the kitchen. Help yourself, so to speak …"

"Oh, hello Brooks Brothers Guy. If you've come for that blow job, sorry, offer's over."

"Look, seriously, are you still interested in painting both of us?"

"Sure, you got some free time?"

"Maybe. How long would it take?"

"How long? Two weeks, two months, two years, no idea."

"Then I don't see how this could work out. I was intrigued at first. But now it doesn't seem like such a good idea."

"Wait, this could be the start of a beautiful friendship, with apologies to Bogie. What if I do start painting you two? You, Brooks Brothers Guy, comes in after work every day you can. If you get sick of it, drop out. No big deal. Ginsberg Wannabe, same drop-out option. Point is, I get started on a project I could really get worked up about. Who knows? What do you say, boys?"

"What have we got to lose?"

"Our sanity. But I'm in."

"Hello there, you the man I used to call Brooks Brothers Guy? Good. You'll remember me as Ginsberg Wannabe. Got your cell phone number from the internet. I'm in town on business for a couple of days. Got some free time? I'd like to meet."

"Boy, I was sure surprised to hear from you after all these years, Ginsberg Wannabe. Good idea to meet at the art museum and take a peek at her masterpiece painting of us. I live just around the corner but haven't seen it since its unveiling, twenty-five years ago."

"Well, I live in the suburbs, a two-hour drive, and I've popped in a few times. So … Don't we both look weird? Switched places since the painting. Time flies."

"Yeah, we're both older than God now. And curious how I traded in my Brooks Brothers Guy look for your Ginsberg Wannabe getup. And you're in a two-thousand-dollar suit. And I never did get that blow job."

"So, today she's famous. And rich. And we're models for the painting that launched her career. You get that thousand-dollar check?"

"I did. Probably a drop in the bucket for her."

"Handy for me at the time, when I was a Ginsberg Wannabe. Didn't have enough money for pizza back then. Fine now, though. Hard to believe I went off and started writing TV commercials? Thanks to you."

"I didn't do anything. You liked what I told you about advertising and you jumped on board. Big time, I might add. Look at you now. Did I see you park a brand-new Beamer back there?"

"You did. If you've got it, flaunt it."

"Well, I don't have it to flaunt. Quit the ad biz and now spend my time writing poetry and novels."

"I know. I asked our artist friend about you. Anything published I can look at?"

"Not really. Just a pile of old manuscripts and a bunch of rejection slips. And now you're Mr. Ad Biz. You responsible for anything that might have interrupted my TV viewing?"

"You've probably seen some of my commercials for Loop Fruits. They're running on most of the networks. And I've branched out into the internet world with a number of software programs I'm working on—"

"Hi there guys, good to see you again. How's life treating you?"

"Hey, what the heck are you doing here, Ms. Famous Artist?"

"Well, I got a call from the former Ginsberg Wannabe next to you. The guy who went from Wannabe to king of the ad biz. You tell him, ad man."

"Right … it's like this, I have an idea for a commercial promotion where we—"

"Wait. You want me to be in one of your commercials? I don't like commercials. Certainly don't want to be involved in one."

"So, the former TV commercial writer is suddenly too good for the real world?"

"That's right, Mr. Richie Rich. Not into commercial, sell-out kind of stuff anymore."

"Yeah, well, how about a little cash infusion to improve your lifestyle, while you're writing the great American novel? Since you look like I used to look. And I assume a paycheck wouldn't do you any harm."

"Okay, okay … I have to say, I am a little down on my luck just now. What are you talking about?"

"I'm talking about a promotion for a product that could change a person's lifestyle. Completely reinvent himself or herself. And all you have do is pose for another painting by our famous artist here. It's like before and after, painted by a well-known artist that people will pay attention to."

"What the dickens is this product?"

"It's a franchise. They're called Reborn Resorts."

"Sounds crazy. But guess I'll do it. Still, I don't like it."

<hr>

"What's this meeting you asked for all about, former Brooks Brothers Guy? I'm very busy. And you've been paid handsomely for posing for her new painting. You want more money to support your writing? I'll see what I can do."

"Listen, I made a mistake. And I think it's only fair to tell you I'm going to spill the beans."

"What the hell are you talking about? My Reborn Resort franchise sales have taken off like crazy. It's a fantastic success. Due in large part to the promotion around that second painting of us that I used in the ad campaign. As you well know, it depicts two people who are reborn. An artistic triumph. An ad man's dream. And you signed a contract."

"You lied, and I don't want to be a part of it anymore. It's kind of like that Marlborough Man who went public with his misleading promotion of cigarettes. Well, I'm going public with your deception."

"What deception are you talking about? My Reborn Resorts are revitalizing the lives of thousands of people all over the country."

"First of all, your ad promotions featuring the two paintings of us by our famous artist are all part of your big fat lies. Like the claim that we're changed because we've been going to your Reborn Resorts for years and using a bunch of your phony Reborn Resorts products. Lies, lies, lies. It didn't change our lives."

"Both of our lives have changed."

"Sort of. But not due to any Reborn Resort bullshit. You made it in the ad biz. Good. But not because of Reborn. And what about your claiming I'm a big successful writer now? All thanks to Reborn. It's fake and absurd. You propped me up. Outfitted me to look like some Hollywood hipster writer for her painting. Promoted me. Published my writing and then bought my books. All so you could lie about Reborn Resorts' success. And now people are hoodwinked into flocking to Reborn. And the lies continue. Well, I'm going to expose you for what you are. I want no part of it."

"You can't do this. You signed a contract not to say anything negative about Reborn. And I'm going to hold you to it."

"Try and stop me."

"Oh, and you don't think I won't? You fucker. Do you have any idea what your asshole scheme could do to my success story? Do you? Listen up, chicken shit, I've got a copy of *Crime and Punishment* laying around my office, and I've got a good mind to put you into the story. I'm serious."

"Really now? The man who used to write novels and poems about people and life and death is now going to do … do what? Kill me? To save his precious business franchise? Well, go ahead. I'm not going to stop you. Really, get yourself a gun or a knife, or whatever. I'll wait right here. Go for it."

"I should."

"Fine, do it."

"I think I will."

"Well, what are you waiting for?"

"I don't know. I really don't know. I mean, I used to write novels and now I'm driving a Beamer and thinking about killing you. To what? To save my ass. To keep from losing a Beamer? I mean, have you ever read *Crime and Punishment?* Really read it?"

"Sure."

"Do you see yourself in his shoes?"

"Of course. Don't we all?"

"I don't know. I really don't. I mean, seems to me there's something wrong with his shoes—and my shoes. Are you happy in your shoes? Are you satisfied with your writing?"

"Satisfied? No, I guess not. Not really. I wouldn't mind trying something different. Something, oh I don't know, whatever, open up a pizza parlor. Is that crazy or what?"

"Crazy as hell."

WANNABE BROOKS PIZZA

LARGE, MEDIUM, OR SMALL, OR BY THE SLICE

"You like the sign?"

"Well, as you know, I voted for BROOKS WANNABE, but since I lost the toss, I'll live with it."

"We'll both live with it. Thanks to two guys who switched roles and switched again and, I would say, finally came to their senses."

"So, do you ever regret selling your Reborn Resorts franchise?"

"I got a lifetime membership. Includes one guest. You interested?"

"I'll pass."

DID YOU HEAR THAT?

"**Y**ou hear that, honey?"

"What are you talking about?"

"A scrape, a thud. Sounds like something fell. Like maybe somebody's moving things around and dropped stuff … somewhere in the house."

"You've been hearing things for days now, dear. I don't hear a damn thing. Nothing."

"Humor me. Please look around. Could be coming from the basement. But I really can't tell."

"Okay. This will be, what? Third time I've checked this month. If I'm not mistaken. But I'll look again, just to go along."

———

"Bill, if you don't cut out the damn racket down here, she's going to find out you're staying in our basement. And that would not be a good thing. Not good at all."

"Yeah, I'm just trying to fix it so I can move around without smashing into junk."

"Well, do it without making any more noise, or you'll be smashing into junk somewhere else."

"Appreciate your help, for sure. I'll keep it down, believe me."

"Last warning. Or you'll be out on your keister. On your own and facing whatever goddamn mess you've gotten yourself into this time around."

———

"My dear, it's nothing. I can't find a thing that might be making any noise, including in the basement."

"Okay, thanks for looking. I must be mistaken."

"Yes."

———

"You can't stay here much longer, Bill. You're my brother. Love you and all. But the wife doesn't appreciate your past screw ups and she doesn't want you around anymore. I know you know this, and surely you understand why you can't stay here. I can only do so much. Get it?"

"I do. Just got to figure out what's next. Like how to disappear from the face of the earth."

"I said I'd help. No questions asked. Because … well, because we're family. And we mean something to each other. I'm wondering, though: Do you want to give me a hint as to what the heck is going on?"

"It's a mess … you see, I did this job for this guy I know. I mean it all seemed like no big deal. Not even against the law, or so I thought."

"What do you mean, you thought? It's either against the law or it's not. There's no maybe. It's yes or no."

"You think? This is a maybe."

"I'm listening."

"So I get this call from an old contact. Not going to say who."

"Don't."

"He says it's a simple delivery. No funny business. I done a million of 'em. He comes over and tells me what I'm supposed to do. Gives me two envelopes. Number 1 scribbled on some scratch paper and taped to the first envelope, and number 2 taped same way on the other. There's a key in both. He says don't mix 'em up. It's important. What he says: 'Don't mix 'em up.'"

"What else?"

"Listen up. He says I'm to deliver number 1 envelope without the number on it and keep number 2 envelope, 'cause he tells me he's gonna be somewheres else."

"I don't get it."

"Pay attention. Then he says he's going to call me and tell me where to send the envelope, the second one with a key."

"Makes no sense."

"Prick up your ears. So I goes to the place told to go to at the time he says. Oh yeah, and we kind of look alike, this contact and me. Anyway, he gives me his hat and glasses and says to me: Wear 'em at the delivery. It'll be dark and pick-up guy'll think it's him, my contact. I says why? And he says: you want the job or not? It was for a good payoff. So I says okay. It's a simple drop-off. What the hell."

"Go on."

"I'm at the place supposed to be at and I wait and I wait. It's dark, like he said. I'm about to leave. Then some guy comes up and bangs on my window and says to give him the envelope. So I gives him the envelope, the one with the key I'm supposed to give him. I stick it out the window. And he, this guy at the window, looks at me kind of funny while he shoves the envelope in his pocket. Then he says he's in a hurry and he's got to go and for me to open my trunk. I says what for? He says he's gonna stick a bonus in there for the good job I did."

"I says what is it? Why in the trunk?"

"He says he wants to hide it for now. Just do it."

"So I do it. And he grabs a gym bag he had stashed on the ground and chucks it in the trunk."

"You see what was in the bag?"

"No. Couldn't see a damn thing. Dark. Anyway, after the trunk business, he walks back, grabs my shoulder and says for me to get my ass over to my apartment, put my car in my garage and leave it there till I hear from somebody. Then he says: Don't go looking in the fucking trunk for any bonus till I find out I got the key what works. I'll let you know. Then he walks off and over his shoulder he says: This key better work. You got your dough.”

"So why is your dumb ass over here and not at your apartment waiting for your instructions?”

"Listen up. I ain't finished. Then I call up this other guy I know what I done other stuff with and say I got a job.”

"What job?”

"I says to him, here's the job: It's to open my trunk. Told the guy somebody put something in my trunk. And I need a witness when I look in the trunk.”

"So?”

"So he comes over. I gives him the key and he goes over to open the trunk. And I don't know for sure why, but I kind of backed up—way around the corner before he turns the key—and then it happens.”

"What happens? What're you talking about?”

"He turns the key in the trunk and the car blows up. That's what happens. It's a fucking miracle I'm around the corner and don't get whacked. But I get really smashed with trash and shit. Stuff blew the hell all over the place. Whatever, I'm alive.”

"What about your buddy?”

"Not exactly a buddy. But he didn't make it. I could see right away.”

"So what did you do then?”

"What'd I do? Got the hell out of there. What do you think? Coulda been me dead on the garage floor. So I call you up. And here I am.”

"You are. What do you plan on doing now?”

"Leave town, I guess. I mean, what would you do? I didn't do nothing wrong. But somebody tried to kill me. Or kill somebody."

"No idea what went into the trunk?"

"What do ya think? Some kind of bomb."

———

"The police are here at the door, dear. They want to talk to you. Have you done something wrong?"

"No, I haven't done anything wrong. Nothing."

"Better not have. Go over there and talk to them."

"Hello, are you Mr. Lenny Lancaster?"

"Yes, have I done something wrong?"

"Not that we know of, sir. We're just looking into a situation."

"What situation, Officer?"

"First of all, we're looking for your brother, Bill. Have you seen him around lately?"

"No, no I haven't."

"When was the last time you saw him?"

"Last time? I really can't remember. See, my wife doesn't exactly want him around … Because he had a run-in with the police. Actually, more than one. You understand."

"We do. Would you mind if we looked around a bit? Just to check on things. And have a quick look at your cell phone?"

"I, I mean no, no of course not. Go right ahead."

"Is there a problem in there, dear? Is everything all right?"

"It's fine, miss, we just want to look around in a few places."

"What are you looking for, Officer?"

"It's only a routine check, miss. Won't take long. And we promise not to make a mess. We'll leave everything the way we found it."

———

"Okay, Mr. Lancaster, we checked your back basement area. Looks like somebody might have been living there. Is that the case? I mean the area was pretty well empty, but some personal stuff was left behind. Kind of messy. Looks like somebody might have left in a hurry. Was somebody staying there?"

"I don't know. I mean yes. My brother, Bill. But I don't know anything about what he was up to. I already told you, my wife doesn't want him around. But he needed a place to stay. And so I ..."

"We understand. And he didn't say anything to you about why he wanted a place to stay? Maybe a place to hide from somebody? We will tell you we found your brother's car. Or what was left of it. There was an explosion. He wasn't in it. But somebody was killed. Do you know anything about that?"

"No, nothing. I don't know anything. But please don't mention this to my wife."

"Not unless we have to. Here's my card. Please call if you hear from your brother. And if we could have a quick word with your wife."

"Wife? Why?"

"Nothing special. I'll just give her my card in case she hears from your brother. Won't take a minute."

———

"What did they want, dear?"

"Don't know. I don't know what they wanted."

"Well, they wanted something. Something about your good-for-nothing brother, I'm guessing. You want to tell me what's wrong? Are you in trouble?"

"No … Okay, I'll tell you. He was here. Bill was here. But he's gone. And not coming back."

"I knew somebody was down there. I don't want that shithead around here anymore. You hear me?"

"I understand. He's gone. Not coming back."

———

"Hello, Lenny? Is that you?"

"Jesus, Bill, don't call me. Stay away. I don't want to hear anything from you or about you, ever again. Ever, so hang up and don't—"

"Wait. Listen to me. One last favor and I'm out of your life. Believe me. And I appreciate everything you done. But I really need one last—"

"No, no, no."

"Please. This is so simple. Only take a sec. Really, one sec."

"What the hell are you talking about?"

"I'm talking about an envelope. One lousy envelope. I left it in my—I mean your—house, your basement room."

"What envelope? Where is it? And why should I give a shit?"

"Listen. It's the envelope with a key in it. One of the two I told you about that my contact gave me. You know, along with that job I filled you in on. He says make the delivery. Just hold on to the envelope with the number 2 on it. There's a key in it. Also, there's a number on a piece of paper in the envelope. He says keep it. It's a key and the number to a safe deposit box."

"What safe deposit box?"

"Says he'll be in touch. And which bank has the safe deposit box. He'll give me his address. I'm to send him the package what's in the safe deposit box. Don't go looking in the package. It's no good to you. What he says. And he says I've been paid good. True enough. Says I'm good for an extra bonus if I do good. Then my car blows up and now everything's a fucking mess. No word from my contact. But I'd really like to get that envelope with the key and the number inside. I mean, sounds like maybe something in that safe deposit box. Something worth something. So, you could stick the envelope in your mailbox. Let me know when and I'll pick it up and be gone. Really gone. Here's where you can find it."

"As usual, you're not making any sense. I mean, where's the envelope?"

"The envelope's in the chimney, one in the corner. Know the one?"

"I do … and then what?"

"Feel around, about halfway up, in the middle. There's a loose brick. Pull it out. And reach in. It's in there."

"Fine, I'll get it. And I want in."

"What'd ya mean?"

"I mean I've been taking a chance on you. And I deserve something in return. I want to see what's in that safe deposit box. And I want something for all I've done for you."

"What safe deposit box? You don't know which bank it's in out of all the banks in town."

"We can try every one of them. We have a safe deposit box number and a key. It has to fit somewhere. We'll check them all."

————

"Hey, how many stupid fucking banks we been to? All with the same bullshit story about your dead grandmother's safe deposit box, and no idea which bank. And we got no luck."

"Shut up. I'll work over here. You try that one …"

"Okay, okay. Hey … Guess what, asshole?"

"Don't tell me. The key works."

"Yeah, it does."

"Well, let's see what we have here … Why, it seems to be a package."

"Yeah, my man. How about we have a look-see …"

"What's the deal here? Some kind of printing plates, two of them. Are these counterfeit greenback plates or what?"

"Guess so. Looks like a ten and a twenty."

"Christ sake, what can we do with them? I don't know jack shit about counterfeit loot."

"Must be worth something to somebody."

"I understand. Listen, you take one plate … Here. Reach in without looking. I'll take the other one. Go ahead and check around for a buyer. You've got contacts. Don't call the house. Call me every day on my cell around noon. Report on your progress."

———

"Hello, Lenny? Got a report. Ain't good."

"What?"

"They called me!"

"Who?"

"Don't know. But they found me. Guys who blew up my car, I guess. Say they figure I got the key, and probably some plates. Say they know I'm not the guy I was supposed to be. He's on the lam. Say they'll find him and finish off his thieving ass. And for me to grab what I got my mitts on and they'll call back to set up a delivery. Say I'll get something."

"What?"

"What I asked 'em. They say not to worry about that. Worry about my health if I don't do what they tell me. Listen, they don't know about you for now. So I'm gonna stick my plate in your mailbox. Hide both of 'em. And don't be thinking about running off. They'll find you. Believe me. Think we're safe for now. Got to figure a way to get something out of this. And stay in one piece."

———

"Lenny, me again. Here's what I tell 'em when they call back. Say I got the plates, which they know anyway. I say they're in a package addressed to the police. If anything happens to me, stuff gets sent. And they don't get diddly. Then I say for them to work out a way to get me something. Something good. And I'll give 'em the plates. But they got to figure a way to make it safe for me. What I say: Make it safe for me."

"And … what'd they say?"

"They'll get back to me."

"What do you want me to do?"

"Hide the stuff. Hide it good."

"I'll get it ready to send to the police."

"Whatever. Main thing is to hide it good."

"Lenny, guys called me. Give me a place to meet. Some out-of-the-way spot. I say no, not safe for me."

"And … what'd they say?"

"They say plates belong to them. They were nabbed from them and they want 'em back. Or else. What they say: "Or else.""

"Go on."

"Here's what I figured out and what I say. We meet at Union Station, five o'clock, rush-hour crowd. I got the plates, you get the money for me. I want fifty thousand. Cash. Old money."

"What'd they say?"

"Okay, but hear me out. I ain't finished. I say, if things don't go right, like if they try something funny, then I'll just drop the plates in the mailbox, the big one at the station. See, I fix it so I'll be standing right there the whole time, casual, while we're talking. And I'm holding the package addressed to the police. And then I say if I mail 'em they don't get any plates or anything. Is that good or what?"

"I guess."

"So: Wrap the plates, address to the cops. Stick 'em outside, in your own mailbox tonight. I'll get 'em."

"Anything else?"

"Here's the good part. 'Cause they don't know you. They don't know I got a brother. Won't know you to see you. I'll get back to you with a date and time worked out with them. You find me. You're standing there, in the crowd, at the station like an innocent jerk. And if things don't go right, I give you a signal and you just walk on by, all casual like. And instead of dropping the plates in the mailbox, I just, quick like a fox, hand 'em off to you, and you disappear in the crowd. Whad'ya you think? Can't lose."

"You sure? These people are smart. And they play for keeps."

"What can go wrong? You tell me."

"See that man with the package, Officer? The one standing next to that open mailbox? That's my husband's no-good brother. And that man in the black trench coat, all slumped over, pretending he's not there, that's my husband. The man next to my husband's no-good brother is holding a briefcase. It probably contains money for his brother. See, I've been keeping close tabs on my husband and his brother for some time now, and I know what's supposed to happen. Now this is what's going to—"

"We know, miss. We've had a tap on your husband's phone ever since you called us, way back when. And we thank you for confiding with us in the first place. So we have this well in hand. And yes, we'll give your husband as good a deal as we can because of all your help. Now, if you will please just go with this officer and let us take care of the situation from here on out."

"If you say so, Officer. I only want to see the … Wait, what the dickens is my husband doing? … Why, looks to me like he raced over and bumped into his good-for-nothing brother. And hold it … The package his brother was hanging onto is, hey, it's gone. Must have dropped into the mailbox. Yes, I'm thinking that's what happened. Oh my, now they're both shoving each other and reaching way down into the mailbox."

"Miss, you stay right here. I'm supposed to look after you, so don't go anywhere. I've got to check on what the hell is going on."

"Goodness gracious, Officer, look around. Where the devil did all these men come from? A bunch of policemen and regular guys. And what are they all doing running toward the mailbox? You better be careful. They're all grabbing and pushing each other around that mailbox.

You could get hurt. Oh my lord, they're rocking the mail-box … Heavens, it's, it's on the ground. The mailbox. Now it's upside down. The mailbox. Topsy-turvy. Everybody's reaching in and pulling. Yanking out the mail. Look at it all. All over the place. All kinds of envelopes and magazines. What do they want? Must want that package. Yes. That's what they want. Hold it. Hold it. There it is. Must be the package. And everybody's yanking and tearing at everybody. All trying to get at it, I guess. Look, the package is break-ing open. Seems like silver bars are exposed. Everybody's grabbing at the bars, and hitting and pounding. Oh my god, was that a gunshot? Is somebody hurt? Lord sakes, I hope not. All seem to be shooting at the silver bars. The plates I heard about. Yes, they're all shooting at the plates and everybody's staying away from the plates. Some seem to be reaching in but then they pull back, away from the bullets, it seems. And everybody just keeps shooting the plates, to keep people away from them. The plates. And shooting. Not pushing and shoving anymore. Just shooting. Look at that one guy. He just shot up in the air. And now he's walking away. Everybody seems to be walking away. Everybody. I wonder where my husband is?"

"Miss. Are you okay? I'm supposed to see you get away safe and sound. That was before. Before all this happened."

"What's in your hand, Officer?"

"That? Oh, that's one of the plates. No good. All shot up because nobody could take them away without, without getting shot at, it appears. So everybody just shot the plates and nobody got them."

"Well, why don't you arrest somebody, Officer?"

"Arrest somebody, miss? For what? Disturbing the peace? Smashing a mailbox? Carrying a gun without a permit? We got the plates, such as they are. Let everybody go on about their own business. Whatever. By the way, do you know where your husband is?"

"Yes, I spotted him in the crowd. Seems to be okay, as far as I can see. And I can tell you, I have a few things to go over with him."

CHAPTER 7

Four Girls Dress Down for Justice

"Jesus, I'm freezing my ass off."

"Well if your skirt at least covered your crotch, might not be such a problem."

"Fuck you. Aren't you guys cold?"

"Of course we're cold. We're freezing. And we're expected to wait in this iceberg of a courtroom, before the workers get here. And figure out our stories. While he gets the heat turned on?"

"I don't trust him. He's a lying dick. Just look at us. Four strangers before he brought us together. All hard up enough to take money from him, a cheesy lawyer to … to do … what? Tell tall tales to the judge in court?"

"I don't know what the hell I'm supposed to tell the judge."

"Weren't you listening to what that shit-face lawyer said in his pre-dawn pep talk to us this morning?"

"I was listening when he called me up last night and said to be here in court, early. And I should dress like a regular Mainer, but also for a judge who has an eye out for the ladies. Makes no sense."

"Great. I assume we all got the same stupid, convoluted phone call. So that's why we're all dressed different."

"Different? Really. Let's see what we got here. I'm looking at one lady wearing a sweater that shows off her nipple, plus fuck-me pumps; another with a pair of L.L.Bean boots and a puffy parka. This one has on a ratty U. Maine sweatshirt and her fluffy Easter Bunny slippers; and I'm wearing a tent-like suit I pulled off a Goodwill rack last night that makes me look like Charlie Chaplin in drag."

"Whatever. So remind us about the show we're supposed to put on, Charlie Chaplin."

"You were there the other day, Nipples, when he first introduced us and spelled it out. Said we should all admit we dated his client. And say he was a real gentleman with us. Everything was consensual."

"I'm not sure it's worth it for the chump change we're getting."

"And, he was kind of fuzzy about exactly how much cash we're gonna get."

"Enough money to replace that junky U. Maine sweatshirt you're wearing, dearie."

"Well, the thing is, I don't think we can trust anything he says, Charlie. He's a pig. Sure, I did the dirty deed with his client. But then the guy got rough, and when I said stop, he just laughed and … he hurt me. Is that rape? Or what?"

"Your turn, L.L.Bean. Did you do it in a duck blind?"

"I was blind all right, Charlie. Blind drunk, and after only one drink that I can barely remember. When I woke up the next morning in a sleazy motel room, he was gone. I had bruises all over me and a wicked sore ass and no idea where I was or how to get home. Okay, so he left me a hundred bucks on the table. Does that make it all right?"

"Hello you lovely people, I'm back, as promised. I know, I know, I'm still working on the heat problem. They're not used to such early-morning starts, apparently. Anyway, looks like I screwed up a bit with the instructions concerning your wardrobes. My fault. Didn't exactly make myself clear. So I got a limo here. I delayed our court hearing. Got just enough time to hustle over to Macy's in the mall, get new outfits for you girls and get back here early enough for showtime."

"You're already looking at my showtime outfit, Mr. Legal Beagle. How about you ladies?"

"Right, Charlie. You can take us or leave us. Just the way we are. Including my nipples sweater and my fuck-me pumps."

"Don't be assholes. You want your money or not?"

"You're the asshole. A money-grabbing asshole. And we're not taking any more crappy orders from you. I'm not even sure exactly what I'm going to say in court. You have the same thoughts, ladies?"

"We do, Charlie."

"Please, please, girls. We need to get our act together. It's important. Real important. For all of us. I'll make it right. What if I arrange to double your expenses?"

"Ladies, I think it's time to negotiate."

"Fine, Charlie. How about we make it triple?"

"I'm going to say we should ask for a thousand apiece. And make our final offer to Low-Life Legal Person. Show of hands, please … Guess it's unanimous."

"Okay, okay. I'm on board, girls. Now, forget about the clothes change. You'll be fine. Except for the nipples sweater and miniskirt. I'll get you a long coat. So: Now we all have stories to tell. And we need some continuity here. You girls know what I mean by continuity?"

"We're not dummies, Mr. Come-On Counselor. And stop staring at my tits."

"I wasn't … I mean I didn't mean to. Anyway, that's why the coat."

"Forget my coat. Fill us in on how it's going to go down. What we're supposed to say. If we agree to say it."

"You better say it or—"

"Or what?"

"You tell him, Charlie. Or what?"

"Calm down, girls, we all need to take it easy and do our homework and get this over with in order to get your money."

"Speaking of money. How about we get some of it right now? You know, before we go to court."

"Good thought, U. Maine."

"Thanks, L.L.Bean."

"I can't access the funds right now. You'll just have to wait 'til—"

"Now."

"You tell him, Charlie. You're good at this. Real good."

"Thanks, Nipples."

"You're welcome, Charlie. And I'll bet my fuck-me pumps that Asshole Lawyer can get that cash now. So we'll just wait here. Cause nothing's happening until it arrives."

"All right. All right. I'll be right back. But while I'm out, start thinking about your stories. Think continuity. Think consensual. Because he's not the bad guy some people think he is. Be right back."

———

"Not the bad guy? Really? What do you think, ladies?"

"Think I'm on the fence, Nipples."

"So am I, U. Maine."

"Charlie, give us some direction here."

"I'm concentrating, L.L.Bean. First let's get some dough. We've earned it."

"We have, Charlie."

"But we've all seen *Law and Order* on TV and we know we have to swear on a Bible to tell the truth. If we don't, it's called perjury."

"That's right."

"So we take the money he gives us. Then we tell him about the swear-on-a-Bible stuff we know is coming. And

we don't want to get to the perjury stage. Because, well …
just because."

———

"Girls, girls, what the hell are you telling me here?
I just gave you up-front money. It's called a contract. So I
did my part and I trust you to do your part."

"I don't think our part should be to tell a lie in court.
We'll be swearing on a Bible not to. Isn't that called perjury?
And what do they do to you if they catch you in the act?
What do they do to a lawyer? You tell me."

"Listen, it's Ms. Chaplin, right? You tell me what gives
here. I paid you all good money to say civil things about my
client. To answer my questions in order to help my case."

"Fine, you tell us the questions you're going to ask
us in court, and we'll tell you the answers we're going to
give you in court. Honest answers. You're not asking us
to lie, are you?"

"No. Of course not. That would be … Never mind
what that would be. Now we're short on time here. Let's
get started. I'll begin with you, miss."

"That's Miss Nipples, what the girls are calling me."

"Right. Now you dated my client?"

"I did."

"And you consummated a coital relationship."

"We fucked."

"Yes. And the liaison was consensual?"

"At first."

"Skip the 'at first' part. Just answer 'yes' to the question."

"That would be a lie."

"Here's the deal, Nipples, or whatever you call your-self. You did it. You said 'yes' to my client. And I would ask you to say that you said 'yes' to him, in court. And nothing more."

"'Yes' is not a complete answer to the question."

"It is a complete enough answer."

"A complete answer to the question, Mr. Cock and Bull Counselor, he started pounding on me. He beat me to a pulp. And that was after I said 'no.' Now, that's my answer to your question. My honest answer. The answer that isn't a perjury thing."

"Girls, girls. We need to get on the same page here. My client is charged with a crime. Unfairly, I might add. I've been asked to defend him in court and it's your job to help me. That's what you all agreed to do."

"You agreed to pay us some money to answer your questions. I don't remember the part about lying. That's against the law, isn't it? We have acknowledged it's against the law, have we not? Mr. I've Been to Law School?"

"I don't think that we're—"

"That we're what?"

"That we're talking about the same thing, Miss Chaplin."

"Charlie is fine. And by the way, what do they say in law school about up-front payment for any kind of testi-mony in court?"

"Expense payments are allowed, Charlie."

"But I assume lying is not."

"I assume you have not thought through this whole business. You see, you have all said yes. And I can make you look bad in court if you're not careful. Very bad."

"That sounds like a threat. What does *Law and Order* have to say about that?"

"Wait a goddamn minute here. Let's start from scratch. I come to you and ask you to testify in court. In return, I offer you some expense money. The exact amount is up in the air. That amount doesn't have to be written down. Or remembered, exactly. And that's not a federal crime. Not even on *Law and Order*. So far, so good with you girls? Nipples, Charlie, and the rest of you?"

"I'm U. Maine."

"I'm L.L.Bean."

"Of course you are. Now, moving right along here. We need to paint my client in the best possible light. Without lying, of course. So if your intention is to send my client to the gas chamber—and nothing else will do—then we're wasting our time here. On the other hand, if you will allow my client a little slack, minus the bald-faced lies, then maybe we can all get together."

"Amicably?"

"That's right, uh, L.L.Bean."

"Good for you, Legal Louse."

"Please."

"Sorry, couldn't help it."

"Okay, here's the bailiff. We're out of time. We need to head into the courtroom now. Not asking you to lie. But there is no need to strap my client to the electric chair. Is there?"

"We're all against the death penalty."

"Thank God for that. Now let's get on with some legal maneuvers."

———

"Ladies and gentleman of the jury, are you ready with your verdict?"

"Yes we are, Your Honor."

CHAPTER 8

DEAD-ON PONZI SCHEME

"God help me!" Gracie Montgomery shouted over the dark ocean's crashing waves. But no help came. Her close-fitting apparel was little help in the biting chill of the November twilight. Thin silk and light knit—all black—suited an evening at home with family or a paramour more than a lonely, frigid beach walk. Her outfit's midnight color extended to the filmy scarf covering her creased neck. Aging had blurred her formerly smooth, sculpted cheekbones, but a Latin beauty remained.

If not from God, then help from whom? she mused. *Her husband, Anthony? Her lover, Wayne? Who, then? Was it her fault it had come to this?* Just that afternoon she had returned from the city to meet Wayne at her husband's showcase

Cape Cod beach house. She was early, thanks to an unexpected lunch cancellation. The day before, Anthony had called from one of his many business trips to Los Angeles. He said Ben, their longtime security guard, thought he had spotted an intruder around their beach house and that Ben would keep an eye out. "For now," Anthony continued, "don't even think about that handgun in my collection, just stay away. It's not safe."

She didn't care. Ben, a longtime, trusted friend, knew full well about her trysts: She paid him a tidy sum to keep quiet. Plus, he was always talking about imagined intruders to improve his value. Her plan was to proceed with what she'd arranged and prepare a special, romantic evening dinner. Anthony was not due to return for several days.

Approaching the house, she was surprised to see two men on the balcony, partially hidden by the potted trees. Was that Anthony? It was. The other? Not quite sure. Could it be Wayne? No, too tall.

The two were talking, gesturing fiercely. She heard the soft crunch of leaves behind her and turned. Then she heard a shot.

When she looked back at the balcony, the other man was down. Anthony was holding what must be his handgun. Her head roiled. What to do? She wasn't supposed to be here. She'd seen something horrible that she shouldn't have. Without even thinking, she turned and ran back to the beach.

———

The next morning, seated at the breakfast table in their city apartment, the early edition *Tribune* front page shouted at her: Man Shot By Security Guard. Gun found on dead intruder at Montgomery beach house. No identification.

Security guard? thought Gracie. Anthony was the shooter, not dear ole Ben, that's for sure. So why don't you phone me, Anthony? Tell me you had a good reason to shoot somebody. And where was Wayne? Why hadn't he called? She needed somebody to talk to, help her straighten this whole mess out.

And that's when Detective Gunther Hurtz called. He came over before an hour passed, sporting stubble on a broad, fleshy, middle-aged face. His sport coat had seen better days. But he carried off the worn, disheveled look with a certain aplomb. After telling her the same story she had just read in the paper, he asked the whereabouts of her husband. When was the last time she had visited their beach house?

Gracie, dying to talk, bit.

"I don't exactly remember, a couple weeks ago, I guess. Anthony called the night before last and said something about an intruder—that Ben, our security guard, had seen one. He told me it wasn't safe for me to go there."

"Yes, Ben reported the incident to us right after the shooting. Apparently it was attempted robbery. Ben said he was making his regular rounds when he spotted a man. Said he had a gun, which we found. Said the gun was being pointed right at him, so felt he had no other choice but to shoot. Told us your husband's in Los Angeles. Talks to him on a regular basis."

"Right, that's where Anthony called from. He did warn me about this possibility."

Then, the detective said, "Now has anything like this ever happened before? Other robberies? Strangers hanging around on the beach? Anything unusual you may have noticed?"

"Well no, actually, this is the first time anything like this has ever happened. We're out of sight of any neighbors, and get very few visitors. We enjoy the isolation."

"Of course. Now you might want to get in touch with your husband. Reassure him you're all right. We'll get back with any further developments."

———

She phoned.

"I'm sure you know about what happened there last night, Anthony … Well yes, I'm fine, dear."

"I know, it's terrible," he exclaimed. "That's exactly what I warned you about. I'll be home in the morning. Just sit tight. Love you."

Sit tight? she thought afterward. *What in the world does that mean? Is my husband a murderer? Or was it self-defense? Should I say something? Or wait and see? I mean, the last time I questioned him about one of his business dealings I didn't understand he, well, he exploded, and out of the blue whacked me a good one. Of course he apologized. Said he was so sorry. And it hasn't happened again. Still. It did scare the shit out of me. And now this.*

———

Early the next morning, Anthony arrived with bagels and cream cheese. As nice and deferential as he could be. His well-tanned, pinched face was short of handsome but still distinguished under a full shock of white hair. He was dressed as usual in one of his custom-fitted Armani suits. "I'm relieved. Imagine what might have happened if you had been there. I think you should stay away for a while."

"Whatever you say, dear." *But I need time,* she thought. *I'm so confused. This just isn't right.*

"Good, now let me take care of the police. You don't have to talk to them. Leave it to me. Oh, and I'm sorry, dear, but I have to go back to Los Angeles tonight, soon as I can."

"That's good," she murmured, her thoughts elsewhere.

———

Detective Hurtz called again the next morning.

"My husband said he would take care of the police. Do you really need to talk to me again?" Gracie asked.

"Just a few more routine questions, Mrs. Montgomery. Only take ten minutes. Clear up a couple of things."

He arrived shortly after with a partner, whom he introduced as Lynda Reynolds, a well-put-together young lady who said nothing and stood back. Hurtz pulled out his notebook: "So, you stated you think the last time you visited your beach house was a couple of weeks ago. And how often do you go there?"

"Well, I go from time to time to relax. It's a nice place to let your hair down."

"Of course, I understand. And always alone? I mean, might you sometimes take a friend other than your husband?"

"Just what are you implying, Detective?"

"No need to get all riled up, Mrs. Montgomery. Only asking. And your security guard did say you always go there alone. But we do have to ask, part of the investigation, you understand."

"I didn't murder anybody, and I think this conversation is over."

"Right, Mrs. Montgomery, but if you know of anything else, I would say it would be in your best interest if you filled us in."

"Excuse me," broke in Lynda, "but there is something else, Mrs. Montgomery. You see, we found footprints in the sand that appear to be from a pair of high heels."

"Of course, Detective. I own the place."

"Yes, we know, but these prints seem pretty fresh, and you said you haven't been there in a while. So, if you're withholding anything, please tell us all you know. For your own good, believe me."

"My own good?" she repeated. "Oh, God, I don't know what's for my own good anymore. OK then, I will tell you both something, just to let you know I'm being straight with you. I'm not a killer. You see, my husband is away a lot with his business and all, and we have this … well the truth of the matter is, we have a kind of open thing. And I do meet friends. I want to tell you this to show you I'm being up-front and I'm innocent of anything criminal. And that's all I have to say."

———

"We need to check her visitor stuff, of course. But I still think she's innocent," Gunther said to Lynda, back at the police station. "At least it seems that way. She's lying, of course. But my gut tells me she doesn't have the where-withal or the stomach to carry it off."

"Yeah? So who'd she go there to meet?" Lynda asked. "And what do you make of that security guard's story?"

"What do I think? I think it's bullshit. He said he saw a gun and shot the intruder from across the room. But the shots indicate close range. The gun matches. The story doesn't."

"Oh, and we got a call from the lab," added Gunther. "Got an ID on the dead guy."

"And?"

"Danny Pitz, a lowlife ex-con from Los Angeles. Don't know what he was doing there. Or how long he's been around."

———

Later that afternoon, Gracie sat in her apartment, still in a state of utter confusion. It made no sense. The phone rang and she answered it.

"Hello? Mrs. Montgomery?"

"Yes, who is this please?"

"A friend. A friend who knows what's going on with all that beach house shit. You know, the dead body and stuff like that."

"Just who the devil are you? And what do you want with me? You need to go to the police. I've got the number right here."

"That's a good joke, Mrs. Montgomery. Real good. That's for sure. So anyway, I'd be willing to meet with you. A meeting that would be beneficial to both of us. Yes, very beneficial. That is, if you don't call the cops. And I'll know if you do."

"And just how would you know that?"

"I'd know, believe me. Now here's the deal: You do realize you're being watched by the cops? Anyhow, I'll meet you tomorrow evening, ten at night, at that worn-down kids' playhouse, the one a short walk down your beach, tucked in the woods. You know it?"

"I do."

"OK, I don't think the cops do. And probably won't follow you on a quiet walk on the beach. If they do, well, I'll have to call with other plans. So, you got it?"

"Wait, how do I know it's safe to meet you, whoever you are, at night, alone? Do you really know what happened? I need to know. It's all too confusing."

"I know, believe me. Saw you that night, by the way. You looked right at me and didn't see a thing. Anyway, you'll just have to trust me. I'd be a fool to harm you. Especially since we both have so much to gain."

———

I should have called the police, she thought afterward. *I haven't committed any crime.* But she didn't call. And here she was in this ramshackle kids' playhouse, tucked in the woods. She thought she had spotted someone lurking around her house during the day, watching, just like Phone Guy had said. But she was pretty sure nobody saw her sneak out through the basement hatch that only she knew about.

"Mrs. Montgomery?" purred a gravelly voice from the other side of the dark door that hung askew at the entrance of the playhouse. "Good to see you. Have a seat, or should I say crate, cause that's all there is to offer you."

"Please don't hurt me. And tell me just what this is all about."

"You're perfectly safe with me," he reassured her. "You have nothing to worry about. And a lot to gain."

"I don't understand."

All that was visible to her in the surrounding darkness was the outline of a slight figure in a dark coat. A wide-brimmed hat, pulled down, obscured any distinctive facial features, but his voice was calm and not threatening.

"Of course you don't understand. But I can tell you some things that'll interest you. And I'd appreciate your help with some details. Like, where's your husband keep his stash?"

"What are you talking about? What stash? I don't know anything about any stash. Are you saying my husband has money hidden away somewhere?"

"That's exactly what I'm saying. And I'm saying we deserve some of that dough. The both of us. Because we've earned it. Big time."

"What the dickens have you done to earn any of my husband's money?"

"The dickens? You're cute, Mrs. Montgomery. So here's the thing: This friend and me, you see we found out—or actually it was him who found out—some bad stuff about your husband. And don't ask me how he found out. I don't know. So anyway, my buddy, Danny, decides he should ask for some, you know, money, to shut up."

"You're a liar! I don't believe you. It's not true." Each protest grew weaker as it left Gracie's mouth.

"Yes, Mrs. Montgomery. But hear me out, I ain't finished. You see, me and Danny are sorta good pals from prison. So Danny sets up this whole thing to get the money. And me, like I'm supposed to be his backup man, says he needs a guy with a gun to watch and help if necessary, which is a good idea, actually. Says he'll cut me in. So he goes in to get the money. And your husband says a few words like 'How's it going, buddy?' and then goes and fucking shoots Danny. Bang bang, you're dead. So what could I do? I stayed hidden, out of sight, to get the lay of the land. Now I'm sorry about my old pal and all. But Danny didn't play it smart. But I can play it smart, with your help."

"Money for what? I don't understand."

"Money to shut up, like I said. Not to tell anybody about your hubby."

"I don't believe you. My husband may not be a choir boy, but he isn't a thief either. No way."

"Sorry to break it to you, but your husband is exactly that. A thief, a crook, a fucking cheat, whatever you call it. And now, like you seen, a killer. And they send guys like that to the pen. For a long time. Or the chair. You see, Danny found out about stuff and he sets up this get-together to make money. And then he gets killed. Anyway, here's the bottom line: When you hear from the hubby again, you're going to say what I tell you to say."

"Now, wait a minute here. Why would I do that? And just what is it I am supposed to say?"

"You listen to me. I can send your husband away for a long time. And he doesn't know me, or even that I exist. You don't know me, either. And that's how it's going to stay. Now, if you don't want hubby to go away for murder, to say nothing of cheating all those loser customers, he'll just have to pay up."

"You're still not making a lot of sense. What exactly is wrong with Anthony's real estate business? He's been doing very well. He has a good name. His company is well respected. All over the world."

"Yeah, if you say so. And I'm not into all the business stuff. But I already told you about my poor dead jail friend, and he said they call it a Ponzi thing. Said he used other people's money to build stuff, stuff that's not really there, you know? Like a castle in the air? And then, more other people's money to build more of these castles. And he keeps going on like that. Seemed OK to me, but Danny said hubby would pay for him to shut up about it. Sounded way too easy to me. And it was. Just lucky I was looking on and not in on the action. But I, or we, can play it smart."

"Well, why don't I just go to the police? Tell them the whole story? Where would you be then, Mr. Smart Guy?"

"Fine, I'll put your hubby away. I'm clean. Saw a guy get killed. And the killer is also a crook. I'll tell 'em the whole story. But you can stop me from doing that. Easy."

Gracie thought for a few seconds.

"What do you want me to do? Are you going to hurt me?"

"Hey, your husband hurts people. He's the guy you want to watch out for. I don't do that stuff."

Gracie contemplated the Anthony she had been seeing lately. "I don't know what to think," she said. "It's all too much."

"OK, let's get down to business. When hubby calls, here's what you're gonna say."

"Wait a minute, before you go on. Did you see anybody else around the beach house that night?"

"Just your pal, Wayne. I know all about him. I stayed around awhile and saw him show up. He didn't see me, but he seen the body and took off, scared shitless. I don't think he'll call you again. Did he?"

Gracie's eyes answered that question.

"Anyway, when hubby calls: Just tell him some guy phoned you and said he saw exactly what went down on the beach. And this guy, who you don't know from Adam, says he knows all about the Ponzi stuff too. That's what you say, Ponzi. Don't mention anything about you seeing any shit on the beach. But that this guy said hubby's got to come up with five hundred thousand. And then, say this guy said he'd shut up. That's all. You're not involved and you were never there. You're just passing on a message.

"So, if you want to cash in, and blow town, fine. Or just stash some away and stay with that killer. You can. Either way, I'll cut you in."

<hr>

"And that's it, that's all I know," she said to Anthony, an hour later, over the phone in her kitchen.

"Don't you believe a word of it," he said. "This guy's dangerous. You be careful. And don't call the police. When are you going to hear from him again?"

"I don't know. I guess he'll call me."

"So when he calls again, tell him I'll meet him. Ask his terms. And understand, these guys are criminals, bad guys who want to hurt me. Guys who don't deserve to live. Can you understand that?"

"I don't know. This whole mess is just so insane. I don't know what to believe."

"Listen to me. Say nothing to the police. We can take care of this whole mess and maybe go away somewhere. What about a private beach house on Aruba? Just the two of us. How does that sound?"

"OK, I guess."

"That's my baby. Now call me when you hear from him. I'll take care of it. Haven't I always taken care of things in the past?"

"Yes, you have."

"Call me as soon as you hear."

"Hey," barked Phone Guy. "Hubby call?"

"He wants to meet with you. Asked what your terms were."

"Tell him he won't see me or hear a word from me. He has to give you the cash. Small bills, old stuff. Then you and I'll work out how to get the cash to me."

"Anthony," Gracie said when she called her husband back, "he won't talk to you. He said you have to give the money to me. I think you should pay him. Let's get this over with."

"Do you know something you're not telling me?"

"I could ask you the same question."

"And just what do you mean by that, baby?"

"I don't know. I don't know anything about anything. I'm just doing what you tell me. And what he tells me. So, tell me what you want me to do. And if that doesn't work for you, well, ask someone else."

"Baby, baby, I'm sorry. I know it's been tough. So just sit tight. I'll get back to you soon."

And he did: "So listen. I'll get a package to you this week. It'll be delivered to a safe deposit box. I'll call and give you the details on how to pick it up. You can tell this to Phone Guy. But I want you to tell me how he plans on getting my money into his hands. OK, dear?"

"What can I say?"

———

"OK now, here's the deal," Phone Guy told Gracie. "You get the money however he tells you to. Later, you're going to take it to the kids' playhouse when I tell you. So, does he know about this playhouse?"

"No, I'm pretty sure he doesn't. Doesn't pay much attention to anything past the landscaping."

"Excellent. What's with this secret door at the beach house?"

"He doesn't know about that either. I had our security man put it in on the sly. It's a concealed ground-level door. I just thought it was a good idea. I'm not even sure why. But it was for—"

"Don't care why. Just that he doesn't know about it."

"He doesn't know. I never mentioned it. And he's away all the time."

"Good girl. Get the money. I'll tell you when we can get together. And if you say anything to Anthony at all about picking up the dough, or anything about me, you'll probably get killed by somebody. Doesn't matter who. If you do what I say, you'll be fine. You get me?"

"I think so."

———

She got the money. Anthony's instructions were easy to follow. He dropped a key off in the mail slot at their apartment. And she took the money out of a safe deposit box at the bank identified in his instructions. It just fit nicely in her second-best Louis Vuitton.

———

When Phone Guy contacted her again, he gave her marching orders. "You're going to be followed wherever you go. So you just go to the beach house for now and stay there a few days. Don't go out till I tell you. Take enough stuff to last. I'll call you with a time and date to meet."

———

Five days later, he called. "Tomorrow night, eleven."

———

She went to the playhouse a little early, but Phone Guy was already there in the far corner.

"Just drop the package off over there in the middle of the floor." He reached over, pulled toward him the Louis Vuitton purse. He rifled through the hefty stacks of bills and counted out the $500,000 into two unequal packets. He handed the smaller one to her.

"Thanks, Mrs. Montgomery. Super work. Now whatever you do, stash that dough away carefully. And take good care of yourself. Very good care. I'm outta here."

She stuffed the bills back into her purse. And waited. *Fortunately, I'm a big purse girl,* she thought.

———

When she entered the beach house, Anthony was seated on the sectional in the living room. "Just where," he bellowed, "have you been?"

"Out for a walk. Why? Do you need to know my every move?"

"No, but I need to know where my money is. Is it here in the house?"

"You gave it to me to give to him."

"No, you cunt. I gave it to you because that's what I had to do. Now I want to know where it is. It's mine, goddamn it. Give me the fucking money."

Gracie recollected the shooter Anthony on the balcony, and the crook Anthony of Phone Guy's Ponzi scheme. Now she regarded the Anthony who spoke to her like this.

"It's gone. He's got it. I gave it to him just a little while ago."

"Let me see that big fucking purse you're lugging around. The one you're clutching like you're maybe hiding something."

He grabbed the Vuitton and ripped it open, revealing the wad of bills.

"Aren't we the sly one? So you were in on the whole thing from the beginning. You lying piece of shit."

"No, I wasn't. He took my bag and he gave it back to me. I didn't look inside. I just wanted to get out of there. I don't know who he is. Honestly, I don't."

He grabbed her by her blouse front and dragged her, kicking and screaming, out onto the porch where he threw her onto the cement floor. He jammed his heel into her back, pinning her down, as he looked out at the beach. He gave a thumb's-down to Security Guard. The one he paid to shoot Gracie. The one Gracie paid more to miss. He turned and shoved her roughly, jumped off the porch and started to run. Gracie lifted her head just enough to watch him through the porch railing. He didn't pause when the shot rang out, so close to Gracie it made her ears numb.

Thank God for my trusty security guard, Ben. Thank God I pay him so well for his efforts. But then, she thought, *you never know.* Gracie's faith in men had been badly shaken.

———

"I don't know where she could be, Detective Hurtz," Anthony said to Gunther and Lynda the next morning at the police station. "I called I don't know how many times, no answer. I'm worried sick. I'm away a lot, you know, so I make it a point to call. Sometimes more than once a day. It's hard being away so much. But my business is such that, well, you can understand."

"I see, of course, and when was the last time you talked to Mrs. Montgomery?"

"Two days ago I think. Yes. She seemed in good spirits. She sounded fine."

"OK then, if there's nothing else, I think we're through here. Perhaps it's just a small misunderstanding. Is there anybody around she might be visiting? A relative or a friend?"

"Nobody comes to mind, Detective. We live pretty secluded lives."

"Well, Mr. Montgomery, please call if she shows up. We'll be in touch with any further developments over here." Anthony looked again at the $50,000 he'd found in her purse. But no sign of her. That was fine. It was going just as he planned. So, she was in on the whole thing from the start. All the more reason to do what he had to do. He checked her cell phone for any IDs he could use to trace the name of that shit-hole blackmailer. No luck.

―――――

A few days later, good fortune came Anthony's way: "Hello, Mr. Montgomery. You're building up quite the list of offenses, aren't you?"

"Who is this?"

"Don't you worry your little killer head about just who I am. But now that it looks like you've snuffed my girlfriend helper, the stakes're up. And I'll have to come up with a new angle. Anyway, I'll call soon. You just go get another five hundred. Old stuff. And I'm not worried about any cops, am I, Mr. Montgomery? I'll be in touch." Phone Guy hung up.

―――――

"So here's the deal, Mr. M," said Phone Guy on his next call. "You take the money, for convenience sake, let's say in a gym bag, to this old kids' playhouse. Thursday, twelve midnight. It's just south, down the beach a bit from you and back in the woods. Drop off the goods and drive away. If you try anything funny, like doubling back, empty gym bag, or whatever, the deal's off as far as squealing. And it's back to square one, with me holding your ace card to the pen, or the chair, who knows? Now I gotta hang up. And have fun trying to trace this call."

Fuck you, Phone Troll, Anthony thought. *I'm going to get you good,* Anthony promised the dead phone.

———

After checking the location out earlier, Anthony kept his appointment at the playhouse. He figured it was probably where his wife's drop had occurred, and that's where he made the new drop. Then he made his way, self-confident, to his car, sure that he'd covered all his bases. He did all this dead-centered in the telescope sight of a night-vision, scope-mounted, high-powered rifle.

Then he was just dead.

———

Phone Guy felt everything was going hunky-dory. As he watched Anthony take off, he was satisfied that this bad dude problem would no longer be a problem. Phone Guy slipped into the playhouse, smiled when he spotted the gym bag, eased down in front of it and started checking things out.

"It's all there," said Gracie, startling him. She stepped aside as Ben appeared next to her holding a rifle pointed squarely at Phone Guy's forehead. "No need to count it. Too bad you won't get a chance to spend it. I don't suppose I could entice you to tell me where the rest of my husband's money is. No matter. It's a small price."

"Wait. Where'd you come from? And I'm glad you're alive. Tell you what, Mrs. Montgomery," he squealed. "Five hundred thousand for my life. Easy money."

"That's four fifty … Anthony stashed my fifty somewhere. But I'm not greedy. We've got plenty here."

"But we're partners."

"I've got a partner, Ben here, my reliable beach house guard," she said as Ben squeezed the trigger. And just as Ben was eyeing the results of his handiwork in the form of a falling, and very lifeless, Phone Guy, he felt a hard slam on the side of his own head. It coincided with the third shot of the day, one Ben was past feeling. It came from a pistol Gracie had retrieved from Anthony's collection.

Ben, thought Gracie, *I know you said Phone Guy was too greedy to trust. You also said we need to clear up any loose ends. And you certainly took care of your share. First Danny, that job was for Anthony. Then I moved in on you with a better offer to cover me, resulting in my fake death, followed by Anthony himself. Now Phone Guy plus his backup. But you were a large loose end, too, Mr. Trusted Security Guard.*

———

"Mrs. Montgomery," said Detective Hurtz in the living room of her beach house, "you've had quite a time of it. First, one body here. And now your husband's shot outside an old, abandoned playhouse, and two more men inside. An ex-con and your security guard. Not to mention an armed man in the woods nearby. Looks like your husband and the ex-con and the man in the woods were all shot by your security guard. His prints are on the rifle. And then your security guard goes and shoots himself with a pistol we found in his hand. You say you were in the beach house the whole time?"

Gracie used a tissue to lift a single tear from her waterproof mascara. "Do I need a lawyer?"

"I can only give you the same advice I gave before. Get one if you think you need one. For now, we're not going to charge you. Do you have anything to add?"

"No. No, I don't, Detective Hurtz. Can I go now?"

"Feel free, Mrs. Montgomery. Feel free."

Oh I do, thought Gracie, and she picked up her big, new Louis Vuitton.

On her way out a casual thought occured to her. *Maybe I should give good ole Wayne a call. A girl needs a man around the house.*

CHAPTER 9

Good to the Last Drop ... Dead

"Empty seat? Thanks. Been awhile. Enjoy your business conference? Must be nice."

"Yes. Only got groped a couple of times. But then, the company sends you away to much fancier places than I get to go to. And they don't grope guys, so you're safe."

"How's your better half? I haven't gotten together with Raymond in … I can't remember when."

"He's around."

"I do recall the last time we were shooting the breeze in the Coffee Bean. And this girl we didn't know walks by, and she couldn't find a chair, and so Raymond just said something like 'You have a nice sit, right here.' I don't know why that sticks in my head. But there you are. I guess

I should call him. Yeah, I'll give him a call, if I can find the time."

"You have a nice tit? Right here? That's what Raymond said?"

"No. That's not what I said he said. You have a nice sit. Sit. That's what he said."

"Well, that's not what I heard you say that he said. And you know something? I can hear him saying exactly that. 'You have a nice tit.' That's for sure."

"Really? Guess you're right. He would say something like that … No, wait, I'm only kidding."

"Well, I'm not."

"OK, I'm not either. Does he say things like that at home? I mean to you?"

"Truth be known, he does. And I'm … well, sick of it. But more sick of what he does. Forget I said that."

"I will if you want. Or you can say more. Actually, I was about to tell your husband I won't be meeting him for coffee anymore."

"Really? Why?"

"Like you said, he's crude. Crude language. Crude thoughts about girls young enough to be his daughter. How he'd like to, you know, do things with whoever. But I've said enough."

"No you haven't. Let me ask you: Has he said anything about, you know, seeing other women? Or girls, for that matter?"

"No. Nothing specific that comes to mind. Why? Do you suspect something?"

"Damn right I do. And I'd like to … I don't know what."

"What?"

"Well, show him two can play that game."

"What are you saying? That you'd, well, go out and do something similar?"

"Please. I haven't done anything since, you know, we were an item. Before Raymond. And I like the way we've stayed just friends."

"Fine. But I have to ask you about the 'sick and tired of what he does' thing you just said."

"I think I already told you that he sort of hits me when things get under his skin."

"No such thing as sort of. And what's this 'under his skin' stuff? You never said anything like that to me, did you?"

"Why should I? We're just friends. Remember?"

"Friends, without once reverting back to how it was before Raymond. And stayed friends throughout all my own hookups, such as they were. Hard to believe we both got jobs as chemists in the same company."

"My lab assistant job isn't exactly what I'd call a chemist."

"You're good at what you do. And you could go further, if you'd just …"

"Just what?"

"Be, you know, more aggressive. Time off with your kids didn't help. Too bad, but it's a fact of life. Fact of female life. Anyway, this sort of hit thing doesn't ring a bell from any of our past chitchats. Must be back of my mind."

"Well, it's not back of my mind. It's front and center … and getting worse."

"Lunch is over. Got to get back to the ole grind. We have to talk. How about tomorrow, after work. Dunkin, 5:30?"

"Done deal."

———

"Hi, table over there. I'll get coffee. Same?"

"Tall, double shot."

"Be right back ..."

"OK. He hits you. Going on for how long?"

"A year. No, two."

"What're you doing about it?"

"I'm doing shit. That's what I'm doing. Shit."

"Right. How bad?"

"Bad enough."

"Did something happen to start it?"

"No. I mean yes ... I guess. He was passed over for department head. Twice."

"That's it? That's all that happened? What else?"

"I don't know what else. I just know he's been abusive for some time now. And the job thing made it worse. A lot worse."

"What do you mean by worse?"

"Just what I said. Worse. I'd really like to kill him."

"What are you saying? Why haven't you said anything to me before?"

"Say what? We were done a long time ago. We talk a lot, yes, but nothing too personal. You know: 'How're the kids? Just fine, thank you.'"

"Yeah, but not the slightest indication from you about any abusive stuff. And I've never seen a mark on you."

"Hits where it can't be seen. Remember, he's a psychiatrist."

"I remember how he used that background to help me address my gender ID problem. 'You're gay, accept it. Embrace it,' he said. But I wasn't sure how. It was like he wanted me gay to get to you. Well, he got you. And I'm out here still thinking about you."

"You are? Why didn't you say something?"

"I am."

"I'd like to leave him. But he's too smart. He'd fuck with me. Maybe even get the kids. I'd like to kill him. He pushed you to be gay and now he smacks me around."

"I'd like to smack him around."

"What do you mean?"

"Just what I said. I'll email you a time to meet."

———

"My turn to get the coffee."

"I like your large, double shot choice …"

"So where did we leave off?"

"You said you'd like to kill my husband."

"Did I really?"

"Were you serious?"

"You know something? If I thought I could get away with it. I mean really get away scot-free. I'd do it. Yes I would."

"Keep that thought in mind for our next meeting."

"My schedule's all messed up as usual."

"Send me an email and we'll work something out."

———

"Let's try that booth way in the back. I'll get the coffee."

"OK, look here. I'm a chemical engineer and he's a psychiatrist. My turn to outwit him. I've got something for you to put into his coffee every morning."

"Wait a minute. Are you serious? Anyway, if I went along, won't he taste it?"

"No. Tasteless."

"Traceable?"

"Very difficult."

———

"Coffee's been tasting very funny. Had it tested. I could put you in jail for a long time. But I have another plan. You see, I have this funny feeling you're in this with your former gay boyfriend. So here's the deal: He quits his job. Leaves town. Never to return."

———

"Listen up. You're going to need a triple shot of coffee after what I tell you what he said to me."

"Fuck. He's guessing at what we're up to. I'll bet he didn't have that coffee tested. I'd say he gave your emails a look-see, found out about our meetings. Made him suspicious. Maybe he saw you fussing with the coffee. You don't have a poker face. But I don't believe he tested or actually found anything."

"Doesn't matter. He thinks he's onto us. Understand, I didn't admit to anything. Played dumb. But he's always asking questions and checking up on me. I thought I erased my emails. But, maybe there's a way to get at them? I don't know. And when he threw that stupid poison idea in my face, willy-nilly, well, I panicked. You think he was just joking around, fishing? Well, he got me. Anyway, he wants you to disappear—or he's going to find a way to put me away. And I think he just might be able to do it."

"He's smart. He knows I work with poisons. But my stuff was deliberately weak. It was a very long-term plan. Let me think about it. Get back to you. Don't worry. I'm very sure you're OK for now."

———

"Listen up. Put this in his coffee. All of it. As soon as possible. He'll never suspect you would try anything so soon."

———

"Thanks for coming down to the station to answer some questions, sir. You say she was an associate of yours from your office. We understand you guys go way back. Close personal friends. If you know what I mean."

"Yes, Officer. I know what you mean. And she was my girlfriend way back. But she's married now. Or was."

"Yes, was. Were you aware of any heart problems she might have had? Serious enough to cause her death?"

"No. She seemed very healthy to me. But why don't you ask her husband? He's a doctor. He should know."

"We did. And he backs you up about her health. However, her husband also informed us that you have access to different kinds of poison."

"I'm a chemist. I have access to all kinds of chemicals."

"Including poisons?"

"Yes. Why? Was she poisoned? Are you calling this a homicide?"

"We're not calling it anything more than a death. Of a seemingly very healthy young woman with a possible undetected heart problem."

———

"I understand, Chief. You want this death settled. ASAP. Autopsy indicated heart attack. No history. Nothing unusual turned up in her system. Husband poured out the morning coffee. Whatever, I'm putting it down as natural."

"OK. Send me your report."

"On its way. I did get a call from the old boyfriend. I'll send the report as soon as I deal with him."

———

"Didn't my wife, before her untimely death, tell you about the deal?"

"What deal?"

"The get-out-of-town deal, you homo."

"You switched her coffee. Killed her, you fucker."

"Oh yeah? Well, my wife is a terrible criminal. Leaves things around. Talks in her sleep. Doesn't know how to properly erase her emails. So I've been onto you guys for a while. I've actually been switching our coffees for some time. Then I thought, why not just send you away? Be done with it. Then bam. She's dead. Just like that. Police didn't find a trace. You're some chemist. I'll give you that."

"Listen up, Dr. Fucking Shrink. You're the one to get out of town. That's right. You see, the body is on hold. Based on my call to the police."

"What are you blabbing on about?"

"I'm blabbing on about a chemical test that I can perform that will show a poison in her system. They didn't check closely enough. But I'm a chemist, a damn good chemist. And I can tell them what to look for. I also think it can be shown you knew the coffee was poisoned. Put you in the homicide seat."

"And what about you?"

"I don't care. I'll take it to court. Whatever happens to either one of us, you'll be fucked. Your career. Everything."

"You're bluffing."

"Fine. You've got exactly one week to decide to leave town or face the music. That's how long I asked the police to hold her body. Said I might have something of interest. If you're still in town, I make my move. If you're gone—really gone—we're square. After all these years."

"Fuck you. You're bluffing."

"One week."

***

"She was poisoned."

"What are you talking about?"

"Poisoned. Old boyfriend told us how to check. And we found it."

"Why not earlier?"

"Hard to find. Needed a good chemist who knew what to look for."

"Husband says the boyfriend did it. Only one with access to the chemicals."

"Boyfriend says husband did it. He knew the coffee was poisoned. Gave it to his wife."

"But, how in the world did the husband know? And exactly what was the boyfriend up to?"

"Lock them both up!"

***

"Who the fuck put the husband and the murdered woman's ex-boyfriend in the same prison mess hall? Tell me that, Officer."

"I … I have no idea. I only know they're both dead. Their lunch companions stated they were both just drinking coffee, got into a heated argument, and then suddenly both pulled out contraband knives and went at it."

"Fine. Check the coffee for poison. As if it makes any difference …"

CHAPTER 10

THE VACANT
MOVIE HOUSE

"Well, we can't wait here forever. You sure you told Belinda the old Guild movie house? Four in the morning? She knows where it is?"

"We walk by here almost every day, for Christ's sake. Maybe her alarm didn't go off. Maybe it's her time of the month."

"Shut up, Frank, you chauvinist pig."

"Sorry. I'm too cold to think straight."

"Forgiven, but you're still a pig. And I assume you being a chauvinist pig is why Belinda hasn't moved in with you?"

"It's this personal thing with her. Won't tell me what it's really about. Why don't you ask her? You guys are buddy-buddy, aren't you?"

"None of my business. She'd tell me if she wanted. Hasn't."

"Right, and my gonads are about to freeze off. So it'll become a moot point anytime now. Five minutes, tops, and you two can go on without us."

"That's not going to work, sweetie. The deal's for four. And we've been planning this winter getaway for, I don't know, how long? How long has it been?"

"My Christmas present to her. Then she added you and Walter, remember?"

"You got a problem with that?"

"Julie please, you and Walter have been our best buddies forever, why wouldn't I want you along? I mean … hey wait a minute! Belinda? What the fuck happened to you? You're all bruised and bloody. We need to get you to a hospital."

"No need, Frank, if you and Julie can just help me into this theater. Maybe it's a little warmer in there."

"Don't be silly, girl. Why won't you let Frank and me help you?"

"You can help by checking one of those doors and helping me inside."

"Do whatever she says, Julie."

"Right. Over here. This door's open. And I've got first aid stuff from my lifeguard gig back at the house. You two help her in. Be right back."

"Kind of dark in here, Walter, but looks like we got movie chairs and some kind of carpeting to lay on. Your choice, honey."

"I'll sit. Just give me a minute to settle down."

"You want to tell us what in the—?"

"Please. Not now."

"Leave her alone, Frank. You heard my lady say first aid stuff's on the way."

"And your lady can do first aid standing on her head, Walter."

"I'll be fine. Just need a little time. If I can only sit here for a bit. Just a bit. Give me a chance to, you know, rest. Be fine."

———

"I'm back. Got the med stuff. And, as you know, I'm the very best lifeguard—a trained pro. Just like you. So I'm going to move you onto this carpet. You lay down, right here. I'll check you out. OK?"

"No, I'm fine."

"You're not fine in that chair. Have you forgotten our med training? Need to lay down. I'll look you over. You're going to tell me where it hurts. Point. I'll have a look. For your own good."

"Be all right."

"Let me do my thing. We can talk after. Maybe think about the hospital."

"Thanks ... I don't need the hospital."

"So, I guess our winter getaway, our cabin in the woods adventure, is off?"

"Jesus, Walter, you are such an idiot. I really don't know why I ever got involved. What is going on in that pea brain of yours?"

"Only kidding. Why don't we find out what happened to her?"

"Why don't you smarten up? What the hell do you think we're trying to do?"

"All right, I admit. I'm at odds here. What's next, you guys?"

"Okay, so my Belinda's out of it. And I'm thinking, when her head clears up some we can take her back to my place. And she needs juice or something. I'll pick it up. Listen to whatever she has to say."

———

"Here's some breakfast stuff, honey. Coffee, juice, toast, eggs the way you like them. Take your time. We can talk when you're ready. About whatever you want."

"Thanks, guys. For everything. But I need some time, you understand. Time to think."

"Whenever you want to talk to me. You know I love you."

———

"All right. So here's the thing. There's this guy. He's not very nice. Yes, we were together for a while. A short while. Short because he started acting strange. Strange and, well, awful. I mean it was kind of nice at first. Sorry, Frank, but that's the truth. Nice at first, then, as I said, it got awful."

"What got awful? And who is this nice but awful person?"

"Not important. A long time ago thing. What is important is that he recently started calling."

"Okay, what did he say?"

"That's the thing, at first he didn't say anything."

"Fine, so how do you know it was him?"

"Oh, I know, from his breathing."

"Just from his breathing, you know for sure?"

"Plus, he has this lingering cough. It was him all right."

"So, we assume he did this to you?"

"Well … I guess. I mean yes."

"OK, let's go to the police."

"I can't."

"What do you mean, you can't? This guy—whoever the fuck he is—is guilty of assault. And who knows what else?"

"I can't. Period."

"OK. You rest. And then all of us go on about our regular lives. Like nothing happened."

———

"So, is this a homicide?"

"Looks like it, Sarge. Found the body in a boarded-up motel. Signs of a struggle, body with multiple stab wounds."

"ID?"

"None. Young. Hippie beard. But prep school dress and looks."

"Cause of death?"

"Don't know yet. Autopsy pending."

"So who are the two couples we just brought in for questioning?"

"We spotted them wandering around the old Guild movie house. Vacant—near the abandoned motel, where the body turned up. Nobody else around. One of the girls showed signs of being knocked about. Said they were unaware of anybody else in the area. Seemed like a good idea to bring them in. Ask a few questions."

"So, miss, you look somewhat banged-up from something or another. Can you tell us what happened?"

"It's no big deal, Officer. My boyfriend and I simply had a little misunderstanding."

"Right, and your boyfriend is Frank?"

"Yes."

"Fine. Now Frank doesn't seem to have any marks on him. Any idea why that might be? I mean, you did defend yourself, didn't you?"

"I guess. I mean yes. I suppose I didn't do a very good job. Because we're fine with it now. No more problems. You can ask him."

"We did. He does indeed back up your story. By the way, will you give us a DNA sample?"

"Do I have to?"

"No."

———

"So, we got a DNA sample from her Coke."

"And?"

"And hers was on the body. And they more than likely went at it. But that doesn't prove she killed him. If I had to bet, I'd say she didn't do it because the wounds were high up on his back—he's taller and the height and the angle of the wounds doesn't work. Then again, the whole case is thrown into a cocked hat by the fact that Frank and Belinda both lied to us about whatever happened to them."

———

"OK, Officer, I admit it. He stalked me. An old boyfriend. Don't ask me why, but I went to meet him. And he beat me up. But I left him alive. Believe me. And I went straight to meet my friends for this winter getaway. We'd been planning it for ages. But then, well, I wasn't exactly in good enough shape to go anywhere. Anyway, we went back to my boyfriend's place and my friends helped me and … but we've been over all this. How many times?"

"We're all done here, miss. Would you like a ride home?"

"No thanks, my boyfriend's waiting outside."

———

"Belinda, I have a feeling you're not telling me everything. Is there anything else?"

"No, Frank. Can we please let it go?"

"Sure. But I don't think the police will, and—"

"Let's not worry about the police, Frank. Let's worry about ourselves. And I confess certain things have come back to haunt me."

"No more questions. Tell me whatever you want. Or not."

"Okay, I guess I do owe you some kind of an explanation. As I told you, he's an old boyfriend, crazy. He recently started stalking me, that's why I didn't want to move in with you. Yes, I agreed to meet him. He beat me up in one of his jealous fits. Then he started crying. Said he was sorry. So sorry. And I left. He seemed fine when I took off. He does have enemies from his dealing days. Something I found out while we were a couple. He got calls in the middle of the night. Bad characters would come around. I even bought myself this little knife to, you know, protect myself. But that's neither here nor there. I finally got sick of it all and bugged out. Then he showed up again here, a few months ago. And I couldn't get rid of him. Asked him to leave. To no avail. He just kept at it. I went over to beg him to leave. I thought I could reason with him. Sometimes you can reason with him."

"So, you have no idea who might have showed up later? The possible killer?"

"No. I might recognize the faces of some of his old friends who used to hang out. Maybe. But that doesn't prove anything."

"Well, why don't you go to the police and tell them the story? The whole story."

"I can't. Just can't. You want to know the truth? I helped him with some of his deals. Truth be known. And if they round up his old buddies, they just might implicate me in something. And then we're talking about possible jail time. Not to mention the publicity that would play havoc with my, shall we say, squeaky-clean image. And any kind of job. I just feel trapped."

———

"Why did you have to kill him, you fuckhead?"

"He's the fuckhead. And he wasn't dead when I left. Least I don't think so. You know I was tailing him to talk about what he owes us. So then I see him and his old cunt-face girlfriend pounding each other. Well, I jumped in and went to break it up. And then I thought, hey, he's the fucker who has our stash, and so I started pounding on him. Weird, isn't it? Her then me. And she's just curled up in the corner. Anyway, I thought he was alive when I left him. Who knew he was a goner? Only wanted to teach him a lesson, couple of punches and stabs to teach him after he shorted us. He said he had nothing there. I said I'd get back. Said he better find something 'cause we want what's coming to us. Maybe that cunt will get blamed.

Be rid of her as a witness for whatever. That would be a perfect ending."

———

"Nice of you to keep the same old cell phone number. That's right, I knew it was you from the start. I want two hundred thou, or you go down. And don't try anything funny. You know your DNA is on the body. And I happen to know the police figure a guy, not a girl, had to be strong enough to clobber and kill him. So, they get your name and a bunch of other stuff that I'm all set to send off if you don't pay me, or if anything funny happens to me—and then you're looking at going away for murder. Leave the money—I know you have it—in our old meeting place. Where we made all those great deals, remember? Day after tomorrow, same place. One in the morning. Sharp. And then scram out of there. I'll get it. Don't you worry. And you might want to think about what a murder conviction could do to your freedom. Or the length of your miserable life."

"You can't be serious."

"Oh yeah! They got your DNA. They get your name and you're dead. You do what I say, or else."

———

"I don't know where Belinda is, Officer. Haven't seen her in at least a week. I'm worried sick."

"Fine, we'll get back with any more questions."

———

"So here's the latest, Sarge. You see we found out what killed our boy. Not all those wild stabs. He was actually alive after those. Messy but superficial, not nearly enough to be fatal. It was one deadly thrust with some kind of a small but lethal knife, after the initial blows, right into the center of the heart, that actually did the trick. Seems like somebody who knew just where to thrust the blade. I'm thinking someone with some medical training. Doctor, nurse, EMT, whatever."

"A lifeguard."

"A what?"

"A lifeguard—wouldn't a lifeguard have the kind of training you're talking about?"

"I guess. Why do you ask?"

"Oh, I don't know. You know how some things just pop into your head. Out of the blue? For no real reason."

"Yes. I think I do."

CHAPTER 11

HOW TO
SUCCEED IN BUSINESS

It was six months before the murder of Carrie Atkins, CEO Robert Meyerhoff's girlfriend. Francisco, a handsome young Latino, was seated in the anteroom of Robert's office waiting for an interview about a promotion.

"Hey there, Frankie my man," said Sam, a coworker who hustled in and plopped himself down next to Francisco. "So, you here to see the Big Guy?"

"That's right, Sam, got a 10:30. And what're you doing here?"

"You needn't get so feisty," said Sam, in a polished tone that matched his smooth buttoned-down look. "Because, you see, I'm here for my own 10:30 appointment."

"'Well," said Francisco, "I'm booked for 10:30."

"Wait a minute." Sam pulled out his phone. "Let me take a quick look at my handy dandy iPhone. Looks like I might have made a few changes to this, and … well, I suppose it could be 11:30, but I am pretty sure."

"I understand, so now you have some free time. Probably see you back here, after my interview."

"That's fine, but I've got nothing really urgent to do right now. Guess I'll stick around."

"Up to you, but I'm not so sure Rob wants people loitering around his waiting area."

"Is that right?" asked Sam. "Do you call him Rob to his face? Seems to me I've usually heard him called Robert or Mr. Meyerhoff around the office."

"Let me worry about that one, Sam."

"Doesn't worry me. Go for it."

"I am."

"So am I."

"Excuse me, gentlemen," said Andrea, a well-put-together, middle-aged woman, tailored by Ralph Lauren, who appeared in front of Mr. Meyerhoff's office. "Mr. Meyerhoff is on the horn with an important call and running a bit late. Looks to me like one of you is his 10:30. And I believe he has an 11:30. Who's got the 10:30?"

"I'm looking at my calendar here," said Sam, "and it says 10:30."

"I believe," said Francisco, in an assertive, Spanish-tinged accent, "I'm booked in for 10:30."

"Are you sure? 10:30 works a whole lot better with my schedule."

"That's fine," said Andrea. "Does it really make that much of a difference?"

"I guess it does," said Sam, as his boyish good looks turned sullen, veering toward a childlike tantrum. "Because I'm more than ever sure that I'm the 10:30. You might want to check your records, Andrea."

"I'm perfectly capable of checking my own records, Mr. Westerfield. And letting you know when you can see Mr. Meyerhoff."

"Oh, of course you are, Andrea. And I'm sorry. It's only because … well, this is an important interview for me."

"That's just dandy, Sam, so why don't the two of you take a load off your feet and I'll let you know when Robert, I mean Mr. Meyerhoff, is free—and which one of you two Young Turks gets to see him first. Or, if you guys prefer, you can just scurry on back to your offices, do something useful, and I'll book you both in for another time."

"I'd really prefer to wait," said Sam, "that is, if you think it's all right with Mr. Meyerhoff. I have a lot to do, of course. But I can always stay overtime."

"There's always," said Francisco, "a first time for you on that score, Sam."

"Grow up, boys," said Andrea. "And I do mean boys. So you two can just sit here and cool your heels all day, for all I care. Why don't I tell Mr. Meyerhoff you're both lounging around on your keisters, arguing about who gets first dibs at him. He can decide which one is more worthy of his time, if he still wants to see either one of you, after he gets the lay of the land from me, if you get my drift."

"I get the picture, Andrea," said Sam. "I just thought of some stuff that could use my attention. Tell Robert, that is Mr. Meyerhoff, I was here, but I'm heading back to my office."

"I am too. And you can tell Mr. Meyerhoff that one suck-up and one worker bee have vacated the premises."

"Fuck you, jerk-off—Oh listen, I'm sorry about the language, Andrea, but did you hear Francisco?"

"I heard both of you," she said as they scampered off. "And you both need a good lesson in corporate culture as well as general manners."

———

"Andrea, here's the thing," said Sam, peeking into her office later. "I'm really sorry about this morning. But you know Frankie and I are going for the same department-head job. Do I have a chance?"

"Sam, I can't talk to you about that."

"I'm sorry. It's just that since you and Robert are, well, you know, pillow talking, I thought—"

"Hey! Who in the world told you that far-fetched scuttlebutt, young man?"

"I have a source."

"I'd like to know that source. So I can usher that source out of here, pronto."

"I didn't mean to say anything that is, well, you know. Does that mean you're going to usher me out, too?"

"Give me your source. Shut up about this whole thing. Maybe we can overlook your rude behavior. Have you told anybody?"

"No, nobody."

"It's not a federal crime, if indeed there is any truth to it. But then, there's no need to broadcast anything like that."

"I'll shut up."

"And your source?"

"OK." He wrote a name on a legal pad, ripped off the sheet of paper, carefully folded and handed it over to Andrea. She unfolded it, stared for a moment, ripped it up, and threw it away.

"That son-of-a-bitch snoop. I thought I spotted her nosing around. You screwing her?"

"Sort of."

"Say no more. She's out of here."

"Can you please keep my name out of it?"

"Don't worry. But keep your mouth closed."

"Yes."

"I will mention that Robert does like you. And that's all for now."

———

"Andrea, that you?" Sam said into the phone. "Thanks for answering my call, finally. What's up?"

"I understand your frustration. But bear with me. You need to show some patience."

"Haven't I heard that one before? Sorry. I've been antsy waiting to hear back from you: Are you about to give me some bad news?"

"Calm down and listen. It doesn't have to be bad news. And remember, you have a friend in court."

"Don't bullshit me with your 'friend in court' stuff. What've you got for me?"

"Francisco got the department-head job."

"Shit! What the hell are you talking about? Where's my interview? Goddamn it."

"That game is all over, Sam."

"It can't be all over. It hasn't even started. I was up for that job. Been waiting, working for it."

"It's about quotas. Robert needs to show our clients that we have a good minority mix. Francisco is first-generation Mexican."

"Is that why he was chosen?"

"You know he's damn good at his job."

"Yeah, and what about me? What am I, chopped liver?"

"You're good at schmoozing and bullshitting."

"What the hell does that mean?"

"It means there's a time and a place for your talents. But you need a push, a mentor, some inside help. I might be able to help you, if you reciprocate with a little assistance."

"Exactly what kind of assistance do you have in mind?"

"I'll get back to you. I have the feeling we're on the same page. By the way, Francisco said he knows how much you were counting on that job. But he mentioned you would probably do a lot better if you spent less time working the angles and more time on the job."

"Fuck him."

"Just saying."

———

"Sam," said Andrea, at a chance meeting in an office hallway, "I need to know something about Carrie Atkins."

"What about that striking young tart?"

"I have a feeling she's sniffing around Robert."

"Sniffing? You mean like moving in on your territory? As in, between the sheets?"

"Call it whatever you will. You're in the trenches. You know what's going on. Fill me in on the gossip, what the troops are saying, and what's really happening. Especially concerning that little bitch, Carrie. I've tried, but can't seem to get close to her."

"OK. By the way, don't forget that little spic has a job that belongs to me."

"I'm looking out for you, Sam. But you'd better watch your non-PC language in public. I can only cover your ass so far. Like when Francisco happens to mention to me that you seem to be busy, busy with a lot of non-company stuff, I'm at a loss as to what I can say."

"Say whatever. Now about Carrie. Yes, she's had after-hours drinks with Robert, a number of times. Sleazy joints, out-of-the-way places."

"That's just great. Robert's two-timing a two-timer. And I can't push her out the way I steamrolled your old girlfriend. Carrie's too high up. Wish I could find a way to take care of her."

"Maybe I can help."

"You've got an idea?"

"Could be, I'm your guy."

———

"Hello, Andrea?" Sam whispered into the phone, "It's me."

"Yes Sam, what is it?"

"Done."

"What do you mean done?"

"I mean it's a done deal."

"What the dickens are you talking about, done deal?"

"Carrie is no longer in a position to be a problem to you."

"How so?"

"Don't you worry about that. Aren't you happy to be rid of a problem?"

"I guess, but I'd like to know what you did to be rid of it."

"And I'd like to know what you're doing to further my cause in this company."

"I don't like the direction of this conversation. Goodbye."

———

"Oh, hi Andrea, thanks for the call, thought you'd get back to me eventually. Assume you want to continue our conversation of the other day?"

"I called to ask if you have any idea of the whereabouts of Carrie. She seems to have disappeared from the face of the earth. Vanished, as in hasn't shown up for work in two weeks. Nobody has any idea where she is. Her roommates, family, friends, nobody's heard from her. I also heard they found some of her stuff somewhere. I don't know where. Do you know anything?"

"No. Why should I?"

"Have you been questioned?"

"Of course. I assume the police have questioned everybody in the office."

"Well, it seems I was the last person to see her, finally got her to sit down with me, for all the good that did. And it happened to be same day she went missing. So the police spent a lot of time asking me all kinds of questions."

"Yes, I know."

"How do you know?"

"I know, Andrea. And I also know you haven't a thing in the world to worry about."

"What do you mean by that?"

"Let's stay in touch. In the meantime, I'll ask you to look into my advancement in this revered company. And while you're at it, you might ask Frankie to stop snooping around my office. He makes me nervous."

———

"Sam," said Andrea into the phone, "they found her body near where they found some of her stuff. What the hell is going on here?"

"Nothing's going on that you have to worry about."

"I don't get it."

"You were with me the night she disappeared."

"I was with Robert, but I didn't tell that to the police because it didn't seem like a good idea."

"I know. Robert doesn't want to be your alibi, but you can count on me."

"What in the world are you talking about?"

"I'll fill you in. Drinks after work today, the Billy Goat."

———

"I'm confused and scared," she said to Sam at a quiet, back table at the Billy Goat tavern. "I feel like I'm in serious trouble. But I haven't done anything wrong."

"Don't you worry. But listen up. I'll tell you some stuff you'll want to know. I won't tell you what you don't need to know."

"That doesn't make any sense."

"It will."

"I hope so."

"Let's start with Carrie. A very, very naughty little girl. You thought Robert was slipping away from you. You were right. So very right. Carrie was in like Flynn. But then she started taking things a little too far. Went for the gold. She knew what the deal was with you and Robert, of course. And that was fine with her. She also didn't care about the wife; if he wanted to stay with wifey, okay by her. What she wanted was to be set up. And then some. So she started in with the threats in order to get more and more stuff."

"What kind of threats?"

"Said she would tell the wife about you, and herself, plus some half-true company money stuff. Inform the staff, clients, whatever it took. Make a stink. Claimed to be preg-gers. Which Robert couldn't prove, one way or another."

"What do you think?"

"Who knows. Probably not. The point is she demanded money. An apartment. A certain lifestyle. No end to it. She was crazy. Robert had no control over her. And that's where I came in."

"So you and Robert are friends? I had no idea."

"Not really. Mentioned what I had discovered, and offered him a way out. He went for it. Had no choice. So first of all, let me say Robert has no idea that we're, like, communicating, and I think it's better that way for both of us. So I spelled out his problem to him. Plus a bunch of other stuff he didn't know about. Stuff on her background. He got a real education. And he got a savior. That would be me."

"How'd you find out about everything?"

"Don't you worry about that. I have my ways. Which include talking to people who have no use for Carrie, and wanted to see her … well, never mind about that. Because that's all you really need to know."

"I want to know where I stand in all this. How can I distance myself?"

"Listen, Robert has been playing cat-and-mouse with you and Carrie, and that left the two of you vying for his attention. The point is, neither one of you has the full picture. But I do. Now, I know you're a nice person, and you were oblivious to the fact she was putting the screws to him. I'm also aware you simply wanted to know what her feelings were, what she was up to. So you set up that meeting. You must have surmised she didn't give a damn what you did. And you could tell she already had her own game plan. But you certainly weren't aware of the extent to which she had her ugly claws dug into Robert. That he felt pressured into playing along or else she could have made his personal—and professional life—a living hell. I knew all this and offered to fix it."

"Oh my God, you certainly knew a lot. So what exactly did you and Robert work out? You're unbelievable. How the hell did Carrie end up dead? How could you …? This is a nightmare."

"Don't you go worrying about what happened to Carrie. It's certainly obvious to the police why you and Carrie ended up together that night. You guys were only talking about Robert. And we both know you're innocent of any wrongdoing. Robert knows he could be your alibi for that night. But he doesn't want to go public with you two being together, in flagrante delicto. With the wifey around, bad publicity and all that stuff. Also, you might want to keep our little pipeline to the top a bit of a secret. Not that Robert isn't ready to give me a little corporate push on his own. But still, certain quiet connections might be best, well, let's say kept quiet."

"Whatever you think, I guess. I still don't understand exactly how, or really why poor Carrie ended up … you know."

"Yes. But that's not exactly how you talked about her just the other day."

"You're right, I could see all along she wasn't a nice girl. And it seemed the whole deal with her was a bit more than just two women after the same man. I didn't feel especially good about the married part—even though Robert said his marriage has not been going all that well for some time."

"Carrie didn't give a shit about how Robert's marriage was going. Or that you were in the picture. I would say she saw you as an asset. Threatened to expose as much as possible. Things that were going on, things that she made up, didn't matter. Eventually Robert saw this and felt trapped. Needed to get out. Any way possible. That's when I came on the scene. I have the whole picture."

"It seems you do."

"That's right. I know all about the goings-on. And, well, perhaps we can help each other out."

"I don't get it. What do you want from me? Will I get in trouble? I didn't do anything."

"I know that. Robert knows that. And I can make sure that nobody thinks otherwise."

"I still …"

"Shhh. Listen to me. I'm going to spell out the details of how you and I met after you left your meeting with Carrie. All you have to do when the police question you again—and they will, believe me—is repeat what you already told them about your little confab with Carrie. What you guys talked about. About Robert, for sure."

"We did. I just wanted to know what her feelings were about Robert. I was upset. Still, I wanted to be fair. I hoped to find out how serious she was about Robert. What she wanted from the relationship. She wouldn't say anything one way or the other. About her feelings, her intentions, or anything like that. It was so strange. I felt, oh I don't know, dirty. Afraid of her. Yes … afraid."

"She was a bad seed. An evil person who thought only of herself. I did some research on her background. Some of which, I'm sure, will come out in the investigation. A lot will probably remain a secret. Robert was certainly surprised when I filled him in on some of the details about Carrie's illicit past."

"Like what?"

"As I said, only what you need to know. Let's get back to that night. Simply repeat the same story you've already given to the police about your meeting with Carrie. Then add what I'm going to tell you. Now listen while I go over the details on how we met later that night. And when they ask you why you didn't say anything about it before, tell the police you didn't want to say anything then because you were afraid it made you look like a loose woman. Get it? And you've got enough of a prim and proper attitude for them to believe you."

"You think so?"

"I know so. Now here's the story: where we went and what we did that night. Perhaps you'll enjoy the naughty tale. Perhaps not."

"Fine. I'll decide on that."

"Yes you will."

"Wait, before you give me my story. How much does Robert know?"

"Not to worry. Robert knows what I'm about to tell you. He doesn't know exactly what our relationship is, as I said. I tell you things. You tell me things. We both come out ahead."

"I think I understand. But it's still very confusing."

"You don't need to worry about the details. Just pay attention to your, that is our, story about what happened that night. OK?"

"If you say so."

———

"So are you and Andrea an item?" asked Michael, a somewhat disheveled, Columbo-type officer who was with his all-business, scrubbed clean, female partner. "Was she your girlfriend?"

"No, that's not what I said, Officer," answered Sam. "What I said was we were together that night."

"And that's fine, Sam. Can I call you Sam? I'm Michael."

"Of course, Michael."

"Good. So you were with Andrea that night. But it wasn't a regular thing?"

"No, it wasn't. She, actually, sort of has a male friend."

"And that would be?"

"Robert Meyerhoff. Her boss."

"And your boss too."

"That's right."

"So how did it happen that you two were together that night?"

"All I can say is we met around 9:30."

"And where was that?"

"My place. We arranged to get together to talk about a business matter."

"And what business matter would that be?"

"It was about a promotion, if you must know. I thought I deserved one and wanted to know why I was being passed over."

"Yes, that's basically what Andrea said. Pretty much the same story. And were your meetings with her at your place a regular thing?"

"No, as I've already told you. This was a personal matter, not something that could easily be discussed at the office."

"Well, we know Andrea and Carrie were observed leaving the bar together about 9:00 that night."

"What are you saying? That Andrea was the last person to see Carrie alive?"

"It seems that way."

"I've seen the newspaper reports. And they say she was found the next morning after having fallen from a bridge somewhere."

"If you read the article, you'd know it was from the Michigan Ave. bridge."

"Right, now I remember. And it seems Carrie died either from the fall or … is there another theory? Are they saying she was pushed, or fell, or something? Like around 11:00?"

"Maybe, why do you ask?"

"Because, as you know, I was with Andrea from around 9:30 on. So if you're thinking of Andrea as a suspect, she was with me."

"Did anybody else see you two together?"

"Actually no. It's not something we wanted known."

"So you both have an alibi."

"Correct, Officer. And I don't appreciate your tone."

"I'm simply conducting an investigation into a possible murder."

"Wow! Do you think it was murder, Officer?"

"I don't know, Sam. What kind of evidence do you think we would need to indicate a foul deed?"

"Let me guess. A blow to the head?"

"Good guess. Did you read that in the paper?"

"Perhaps."

"Perhaps not."

"Why do you say that?"

"Because it wasn't in the paper."

"Fine, that doesn't prove a damn thing."

"Right, so does Robert Meyerhoff know you and Andrea were together that night?"

"I have no idea. You'll have to ask him."

"We did, and he says he doesn't know where Andrea was that night. He was home. His wife backs him up."

———

"I'm trying to piece these stories together," said Officer Michael, "and they don't quite fit."

"You got that right," said his partner. "And I wouldn't know where to start."

———

"I'm going to the police, Sam," said Andrea. "And tell them I didn't do anything. Get rid of all the lying. Tell them where I really was that night. And that I feel I need to wash my hands of the whole thing. I don't know exactly what you did. Well, I sort of know, but I really don't want to know any of the details. That's for you to go over with the police, or whoever. But I'm beginning to understand some things. You seem to have Robert and me under your thumb. It's almost like you've pulled a 'Carrie' on Robert, and you've managed to put me into the same fix. Like you planned out the whole thing ahead of time. Control Robert, control Andrea, through blackmail."

"Now you listen up here. You have no idea how much trouble you could be in, unless you decide to play ball with me. You could fuck up everything. Life as you know it would be all over, baby. The end."

"What do you mean?"

"I'll tell you what I mean. And then you can make a big decision: a life down the tubes, or one free and clear of bad shit. It's up to you, dear. Actually, you and Robert. That 'tell the police' bullshit you're into, you guys are suddenly a sweet little team. But it was a possibility I anticipated. And planned for. Just in case."

"I don't get it."

"Here's the thing. Spill your guts to the police," he said, "and you've just lost your original alibi. We're told that Carrie fell, or whatever, off that bridge around 11:00 p.m., so now you guys would be each other's brand-new alibi. And listen to this little factoid: Both of you have your DNA all over Carrie. That's right. Could be explained away, sure. But all of sudden, you guys could be made to look very bad. And by the way, my DNA is not anywhere around her. No sir. And if it comes to it, which I'm not sure it ever will, I do have an alibi. Because, just like you, I did nothing wrong. So now, following this little story line, you two are the only suspects that I see on the crime-scene horizon."

"But I didn't do anything."

"Of course you didn't. And perhaps you'll both be cleared of murder. I have this funny feeling that this will all end neatly for you. But … let's say it was murder, and after all the investigation brouhaha, you guys are, hopefully, cleared. There's still all that publicity that would probably not be very good for Robert's company. Not very good at all. Might even put it under. Which would be a shame. A damn shame. After all that work. Like getting the right minorities into the right places to look good for all those liberal-minded clients. Then there are the bullshitters, like me; you need them too, don't you?"

"Perhaps."

"Anyway, it's something to think about. Your future. The company's future. So you just run it up the ole flagpole. And then go to the police, if you must. You might want to talk it over with Robert first, though. By the way, I already have."

———

"The stories don't add up, do they?" Officer Michael said to his partner. "Sam spending the evening with his boss's girlfriend, out of the blue. Ending up as each other's very convenient alibi. Then of course we have the DNA traces for Robert and Andrea found on Carrie. All over. But, you know that could be explained away in court by a good lawyer. And not prove a damn thing. If indeed it ever goes that far, which I'm doubtful it ever will. If it did, I suppose it would make for good press, if you're into that kind of dirt-bag journalism."

"Then there's Sam. He is an odd duck. Wouldn't you say?"

"Yes, that's for sure."

———

"Andrea," said Francisco over the office intercom, "I need to see you and Robert. His office."

"Anything special?"

"It's about Carrie."

"I'm not so sure …"

"You both better be there. I'll be right over."

———

"Francisco," said Sam, "please don't come into my office. I'm sick and tired of you stalking me."

"Sam, say hello to an old acquaintance of yours: Officer Michael. You'll remember him from your previous interview at the police station."

"We've met. Get out of here."

"Bad move, Sam. I'm the one out of here. And I strongly advise you to listen to the police officer."

"I must tell you, Sam," said Officer Michael, "this is about the Carrie Atkins homicide investigation. Now you have a perfect right to call your lawyer. He knows about this meeting. And he says, as long as you don't say one word to me, you're all right. I'm simply going to lay out a few facts. No questions, no answers required. When we're done here you go ahead and talk to your lawyer and make a few decisions. Are you OK with that?"

"Wait. I've been cleared, haven't I?"

"So far. But since then, Francisco has come to us with a few suggestions for further investigation based on his observations of certain comings and goings in your office. Just listen. OK?"

"You can't accuse me of anything."

"I'm not. Hear me out. First, your lawyer wants us to assure you that all the facts we'll be presenting are still only circumstantial evidence."

"So, no good in court?"

"Sometimes yes, sometimes no. It's a gamble. One you'll soon learn about."

"I don't like this."

"Francisco came to us. We in turn interviewed Robert and Andrea. They are ready to confess to aiding and abetting."

"I don't understand. What will happen to them?"

"Can't say. Hasn't gone to court. Just let me lay out the facts. Again, your lawyer wants me to remind you we're talking circumstantial. OK now, Robert's and Andrea's DNA was on Carrie Atkins's body. It's possible a case might be made that it could have been planted. Your DNA was not present directly on the body. But there are slight traces …. possibly scrubbed away. Your lawyer wants me to tell you there is not enough of this DNA to hold up in court. But understand, your alibi no longer holds water. Also, your lawyer wants me to assure you we can't positively place you at the murder scene. You'll want to review with your lawyer a few points. DNA, or lack there of, testimony from Robert and Andrea. Observations of Francisco. You have a decision to make."

———

"Francisco," said the receptionist over the intercom, "man out here in your anteroom says he's a policeman.

Wants to see you. But he's not in uniform, Should I send him into your office?"

"Please do."

"Francisco," said Officer Michael. "I won't be long. As the new CEO here, you must be busy."

"Yes. And thank you for coming in plainclothes. As I said, I want this whole homicide thing kept as quiet at possible."

"Understand. I just want to drop off this official letter of commendation from the mayor for your help in the investigation. Along with his congratulations on the board of directors appointing you the new CEO."

"Thank you. And they also appreciate the absence of bad publicity for the company."

"Not easy. But we managed."

"So no news is good news, but I am curious as to the fate of certain former employees."

"Nothing certain. Trial upcoming. No jury. Judge is about to rule on a plea bargain for Robert and Andrea. I'd say five years, most of which will be suspended. Sam weighed his options. His lawyer said a trial could mean life without parole, or freedom. Crapshoot. A plea deal probably come to ten to fifteen, time off for good behavior. Word is he's going to take the plea."

"Justice, I guess."

"So, what's your first move as CEO?"

"Please keep it quiet, as I know you can. But I'm appointing a new assistant. A number two man. Actually a woman. Can't say who yet, but she's of Mayflower descent.

So basically, we'll have descendants of both settlers and natives running the company. Gives us a good majority/minority mix—great for our image."

CHAPTER 12

The Drug Trade: A Philosophical Approach

"One good thing about my broken leg is I don't have to ski for a while—make that never again …

"Take up skiing, that's what my friend Brenda said. For sure I'd meet guys. Well, I don't like skiing, I met a bunch of full-of-themself losers and now I'm hobbling around on this stupid cast from my skiing accident. Plus, my building's elevator here is taking forever. Shit, the floor indicator needle isn't even moving. Does that mean it's broken? Yes, you asshole. And it's only the third time this month. Not a problem. Merely a ten-flight walk-up. On crutches. With a cast. Guess I'll just plop myself down here on these stairs, set up camp in the lobby, call for takeout food, order a bedpan for when nature calls."

"Excuse me, miss. Can I help you? You see, I need this area you're sitting on cleared out for some repair work."

"That mean you're going to fix the elevator?"

"Elevator? No. I don't know anything about your elevator. See that water in the corner? It's coming up from somewhere. I was sent to check it out. Find out where the problem lies. And I wouldn't recommend you stay on these stairs, with your cast and all. I need to look right under where you're seated for any leaky pipes."

"Fine. So where would you like me to sit?"

"Sit wherever you want. Except not right there."

"Most everything else is wet. This floor's been wet ever since I've been a tenant here."

"So where're you headed?"

"Where am I headed? How about to my apartment?"

"And exactly where would that be, miss?"

"That would be number 1027. That's on the tenth floor. And I'm not sure I'm up to maneuvering cast and crutches up quite that far."

"I can see your problem."

"Can you really? So they teach you how to see problems in plumbing school."

"I deserve the sarcasm, miss. Actually, I'm a philosophy grad. But not many job openings in my field. So here I am. And here you are."

"More insight into my problem. Is a solution forthcoming, Mr. Philosophy?"

"Look, if you can just scrunch over a bit, maybe I can get at those pipes …"

"Okay … here goes … am I out of your way? I can only move so far."

"Looks good, I'll just pry open this stair board … reach down here … slide this pipe over a tad so I can have a peek. And then maybe give this valve a little twist … shit."

"Hey, I'm getting soaked. What in the world do you think you're doing?"

"Damn it to hell, I have no idea what the dickens happened here. It won't turn off. Maybe I should have closed the main valve first."

"Maybe you should check out the waterfall that's soaking me and help me out of here before I drown."

"I don't see how I can do both at once. Here, let me carry you over there … Watch out for that gush. Christ, I need some help with this."

"Just let me down … No, not here, it's all black water."

"How about this stoop? Is that better?"

"Sort of. It's all relative, I guess. Isn't there anybody you can call?"

"I'm thinking … This can't be happening to me."

"Fine, what about me?"

"Right, we need to figure out a way to get you to your apartment. Ten flights up?"

"That's right, Mr. Philosophy. Up."

"Maybe I can lift you and carry … no, that's not going to work. Hey, how about an EMT? Don't they move people around on stretchers and stuff?"

"They move them to the hospital. Not to their apartments."

"Yeah. So, you have any suggestions?"

"How about calling someone? Anyone, like somebody at your office. And ask that person to come over here and turn off the water. Or bring over a rowboat before the water reaches the second floor."

"Hold it. The elevator door is opening."

"Splendid, and I can see water is flooding out the door. Want to try it out?"

"I guess not. I'll call my office. I'm not really sure what to tell my boss. I don't exactly get along with her."

"That's just great. Want me to talk to her? Give her the lay of the land. Make that lay of the water."

"Very funny … Hello Elizabeth? It's me, Maury. Look, I'm at that apartment job about the water leak. You know the one? Right. Well, I need some help … You say everybody's out over there? Listen, I really need some help here. Now. See, water's all over the place. I mean everywhere. No, I can't call back … I don't believe it. She hung up."

"Wonderful, call 911, the police, the fire department, anybody who might help. Can't you see the water's gushing out the front door? Wait—looks like there's a bunch of people out there. I suppose they're all wondering what the heck is going on in here."

"Hey, is that a fire truck?"

"Thank God. Does that mean the end of this nightmare?"

———

"Well, Mr. Philosopher, I'll be honest. When you called me, my first reaction was to hang up. No, it was actually to cuss you out, and then hang up."

"So, why didn't you?"

"I don't know. Guess I felt sorry for you. Realized you found yourself in an awful pickle. Not your fault. Sort of. Anyway, when you asked me out for dinner, I thought, why not? What have I got to lose?"

"Exactly."

"Well, we both seem to be losers, don't we? You're probably out of a job as a plumber. I can't do the traveling needed for my pharmaceutical sales job. And I don't think they're going to hire me back. Bummer."

"Why don't you think they'll hire you back?"

"Well, I sold some drugs. And somebody told them about it."

"Isn't that's what you do?"

"You see, it was, like, under the table. Sort of."

"You mean you stole stuff and sold it."

"No. Not exactly. Actually, I paid for the drugs and then sold them."

"So, what's wrong with that?"

"It's complicated. You're supposed to have a prescription. And I got them cheap, like from people I know who work at the factory, and, well, you get the idea."

"I guess I do. You still in touch with those people?"

"Well, yeah. Why?"

"Where's their factory?"

"The factory? It's in Mexico."

"So you smuggled drugs in from Mexico?"

"That sounds so crass. But yes. That's basically what I did. But only in small amounts. And only for a little while."

"How'd you do it?"

"How? I just stuck small amounts in my bra."

"And now you're in a cast."

"What's your point?"

"A cast is bigger than a bra. Both of our jobs are in doubt. And I could use a bit of financial assistance. How about you?"

"Yes, Mr. Philosopher. So you think the contents of one cast will produce a windfall? I mean, I can't keep going back and forth. They'll start asking questions. And anyway, what do you bring to the table?"

"I'm not sure. Let's get off this subject. Finish our dinner in peace and quiet. But you've given me something to think about. And if you don't mind, I'd like to get back to you with some ideas."

"I guess, but I'm not at all sure I'm going to like any of your ideas."

"We'll see."

———

"So, we meet for another fun-filled dinner date. And how's the broken leg doing?"

"It's doing."

"And the apartment?"

"Elevator's working. Your replacement fixed the water pipes. You must be out of a job."

"I am. You?"

"Same."

"So that's what I want to talk to you about."

"I was afraid of this. Look, I'm not interested in being any kind of a drug lord. I mean, they put people in jail for that kind of stuff."

"I know, I know. But hear me out. I've done some homework."

"I'm sure. But I'm not about to stuff any more little bags of drugs in my bra."

"Fine, but think about big bags in a big cast."

"Not going to put stuff in my cast either."

"Not your bra or cast. Somebody else's."

"Whose? What are you talking about?"

"I'm talking about different people going back and forth. Different young people with casts and crutches and bras and other stuff."

"And just where are you going to get all these different young people?"

"College campuses. I'll recruit them. I've already started checking around. I have lots of connections from grad school."

"Your name will get out. Somebody will turn you in."

"If we just reach out two, three, four, or even more, levels in recruiting, we can stay in the background."

"Well, some are bound to be caught."

"Yeah, but a few catches are small potatoes. A fine, a slap on the wrist, whatever. And we stay way in the background. Be impossible to trace anything back to us. If we're careful."

"Where did this all come from? I mean, we're out on a casual dinner date and all of a sudden we're a big-time drug cartel."

"I don't know. I really don't. It all came to me after you told me what you were up to with your sales job."

"Just like that? Out of the blue?"

"I'm a philosophy grad, out of a job, out of money. And I start philosophizing on the business side of things. Are you in?"

"Let me think about it. Maybe. But I really don't like it."

"Excuse me guys, you have a minute?"

"Where'd you come from?" Mr. Philosopher asked. "This is a private residence."

"I'm looking for a job."

"I don't know what you're talking about. We're not an employment agency."

"Oh, yes you are. And let me tell you, it took me a long time and a lot of legwork to find you guys."

"Get out of here."

"You better listen to me. I know about your operation. I actually worked for you for a while. A mule, as perhaps you call us. And I started looking around for a source, a leader of the band, so to speak."

"I'm going to call the cops."

"Not a good idea."

"Listen, feminine intuition tells me we should give her a hearing," chimed in his partner.

"All right," he agreed. "Speak up, asshole. What makes you think you know so much?"

"Oh, I know a lot. I know that she was fired from the same pharmacy company we both worked for. And I know why she was fired."

"Are you the one who squealed on me?"

"No. But I know who did and all about the whole deal. Or enough. Anyway, I was recruited and started working for you guys. And it was fine at first. Except: small-time pay for big-time risk. Then I discovered, quite by accident mind you, the name of your Mexican supplier. And I knew, from personal experience, it was the same supplier for your old, penny-ante smuggling operation. And then it all came together; I traced everything back to you. And your new partner, whoever the hell he is."

"Just what is the point of this bullshit story?"

"My point is, I think you need another partner."

"Just like that. Simply because you think you know something. You want in?"

"Hey, a mere pittance. You guys are making out like gangbusters."

———

"We're never going to be rid of her. She found me and she'll follow us to our grave."

"What about her grave?"

"What are you saying?"

"What do you think I'm saying? We're paying her off to keep her quiet. And she keeps coming back asking for more and more. You want to continue putting up with that crap?"

"I think I know what you're driving at. But I just can't be a part of anything like what I assume you're suggesting."

"We're not going to be a part of anything. But our supplier is a drug dealer who does things like that. Especially for good customers. And we're a good customer."

———

"Our gringo client called. He wants us to take care of a lady who he says is blackmailing them. He doesn't understand. We don't get involved in that kind of stuff. No way."

"I never did trust those guys. Fuck 'em, we can live without 'em. I say we warn the lady in question, and then call the Americano cops and fill them in on the operation. They can't do anything to us. We'll be rid of those flaky gringos. And out from under any really bad gangster jobs."

———

"I'll tell you something, Sergeant. And it's so weird. We got a call from this drug dealer type in Mexico. He says they were asked to get rid of a lady who was blackmailing one of their 'supposed' clients. Said they didn't want to be part of anything that bad. Yeah, said they may, or may not, have had some dealings with drugs, which we can't prove anyway. He said they didn't want to be connected to things like killings. Said they wanted to stay clear of that sort of business. They had their standards."

"Yeah, yeah, so exactly what did he tell you?"

"He gave us the name of the woman they were supposed to do in. She is apparently shaking down an American couple these Mexican guys have dealings with. So we contacted the lady in question, told her what we know. She acted surprised and really scared. And eventually verified the names of the couple we were told she was actually blackmailing. So, we called on this couple who is apparently running some kind of a smuggling operation. Thing is, with all this talk and name-calling and accusations, here and in Mexico, we can't pin a damn thing on anybody."

"Right, what's your point? What the heck do you want to do? Drop the whole thing or what?"

"I have this crazy idea as to how we might put this whole stupid thing to bed."

***

"Okay, is everybody ready?"

"Yeah, we're all set down here in Mexico."

"And we're both on board, up here in the States."

"I'm in the States too. Can't tell you where."

"Looks like we're all set to go. Thing is, as we told you people, our police department has set up a Zoom call to your three Zoom locations. Now, first you in Mexico. You're the guys who initially called us with an inside tip that started the ball rolling. And then there's you, Stateside lady. We understand you're the woman who is supposedly working some kind of shakedown. And then there's you two, the couple who are being blackmailed. Perhaps working a smuggling deal."

"Wait a minute, you said nothing about smuggling would come out about either of us. You promised—"

"Right, and you guaranteed everything would be on the QT about my supposed shakedown—"

"And you came on to us in Mexico about how none of our what you call our 'dealings' would come out. We want to stay good, people."

"Listen up, everybody. Believe me. As we promised all of you, none of your names will be used. Let's label this call a 'get-together' meeting. Yes, you're on Zoom, but your faces are obliterated. And none of our conversation is on tape. Trust us. We only want to start with a clean slate. Understand, we have no proof of any wrongdoing. And we're not going to go looking for any. So let's get started."

"You're a gringo. Not to be trusted."

"I'm the one who was targeted. How can I be sure I'm safe?"

"I thought shakedowns were illegal. Will we be free of anything like that in the future?"

"Pay attention, please. Nobody's going to be prosecuted. Nobody's going to jail because of us. But we're asking each of you, for your own sake, to follow a few suggestions. First of all, the shakedown girl. It's all over. Go on about your own business. And get out of the blackmail profession. Because if you're caught again in anything that resembles this mess—well, it will go down hard on you."

"Yes, yes, I understand."

"We hope so. Next, the couple who started a very, very bad business. Perhaps involved in moving things where they shouldn't be moved. Understand, it will be the end of life as you know it, if you try the same line again."

"We both made a mistake. You see, we both thought that if we—"

"It doesn't matter what you thought then. It's what you think now."

"Okay, Mexico. Your turn. As you're certainly well aware, we have nothing on you now. And we do appreciate you steering clear of any really bad activity. And calling us in the first place. Now, we are advising you to stay clear of certain types of business ventures. But then again, that's your decision. We will, of course, continue with our jobs as you will, more than likely, continue with yours. Whatever that may be."

"We got our business down here. You got yours up north. Maybe we'll meet again. Better if we don't. Ain't that right?"

"I think so."

CHAPTER 13

Don't Jump to Deadly Conclusions

Robert could have avoided a deadly outcome if only he had remembered to take his wallet with him. The oversight was discovered as he went to pay for his morning coffee before heading up to his newly acquired corner office. Yes, on his way up in the corporate world, he gloated. He had certainly worked hard enough for it. Perhaps at the expense of some everyday responsibilities like, say, his marriage. But he was now the company's chief financial officer. And if he stayed with it, who knows what great things might follow. Then again, he wondered whether great things follow people who forget their wallets.

Nothing left for him to do now but hustle out of the coffee shop, make a beeline for the parking lot, spend more time on the damn interstate, drive up to his front door, walk through the entrance and on up to his bedroom. The one that he suddenly discovered had more than one occupant. Both of whom were engaged in a very inappropriate, intimate activity.

Fuck the wallet. Fuck, fuck, fuck. I'm out of here, he agonized. He was now on the interstate yet again. Not worried about his wallet this time. He was worried about another matter entirely. What he knew and didn't know. He knew Anthony Rutledge, the company's CEO and his boss, was in that bedroom. He recognized his briefcase in the hall. He didn't know if his promotion was related to this … this situation. This state of affairs, if you will. Or what he should do about it, if anything.

I could kill him, he thought. *Be a crime of passion.* He wasn't so sure the jury would see it that way. He considered killing him anyway. Yes, he'd been neglecting her. But mainly because of the workload he'd been given by Anthony. Overtime galore, weekends, out-of-town assignments. And his reward? A new office and a new title: cuckold.

"Mr. Rutledge?" Robert said at the last-minute meeting he had asked for.

"How many times have I asked you to call me Anthony?"

"Keep forgetting, Anthony."

"What can I do for you, Robert?"

"Well, this is the third week in a row you've given me an out-of-town assignment … Anthony. Couldn't one of my staff handle this latest piece of business in Boston?"

"Need the head money person to work on this one, Robert. They requested you, Robert Stiker, in person. You should feel proud. You'll be working with Joseph Marvo. Meanwhile, I'll try to ease up on the load on your department. Perhaps an assistant would help?"

"Sure would. Is that a promise?"

"Ha, ha. Don't push it, Robert. But I'll make sure to put it in the ole pipeline. And I know you'll do a good job in Boston. Don't worry about the expense account; this guy likes to be wined and dined."

"I'm always careful with expenses, Anthony."

"I know. Appreciated. One more little matter. Hints of a Mafia connection here. They once asked us to overlook a certain monetary situation. We refused. Water over the dam. Not to worry. The company Joseph represents likes us because of our squeaky-clean reputation. You're as safe as can be with them. The firm came on board a short time ago. Major addition. If you get my drift."

Oh, I do. I certainly get it, Anthony, he thought. *Do you? is the question.*

"Good to be home, love. You know something? I forgot my wallet this morning."

"Oh dear, how did you manage? Was it a problem? I don't know if I could get by without mine."

"Well, I almost came back for it."

"Is that right? So why didn't you? I mean, you didn't—"

"No, figured I could muddle along. And I did. Muddle along. Borrowed some from my secretary. Muddle, muddle, all worked out."

"That's nice, dear. I'll try to remember for you in the future."

"That's a good wife, thank you."

"You sound a bit out of sorts. Is something besides your wallet bothering you?"

"Not at all. Why do you ask?"

"It's not like you to forget your wallet."

"Tell me about your day, Sophie. All of it."

———

"Sophie, please don't call me at the office."

"Sorry Anthony, but Robert's acting funny. Anyway, why can't we get away for a while? Stop this quickie stuff at my house. I could say I'm visiting my sister. You could do some out-of-town business, whatever. We both need a break."

"Not now. Bad timing. Perhaps we should lay low for a while."

"Lay low? What are you talking about? What happened to our divorce plans and long-term arrangements?"

"Can't talk now. Later. And don't call me at the office."

———

"So, it's been a productive week, Joseph. I've enjoyed learning about your company. Your numbers are certainly impressive. And as I pointed out, the numbers could be made less impressive, if that's something your company might be looking for."

"Yeah, I'm a direct kind of guy. What's your point?"

"You've asked us to jigger your numbers before. We've said no. We're squeaky clean. That's why you're with us."

"Get to it."

"Well, I don't know anything concerning rumors around your company's connections. I do know a lot about numbers. And I have this crazy idea."

"Yeah, I'm all ears."

———

"Robert, wake up! Look at the *Press Herald's* online news this morning."

"What time is it? What're you talking about?"

"Paper says Anthony is dead. Says he fell from the roof of his office building. I mean, he certainly didn't jump."

"Anthony who? And why are you so sure he didn't jump?"

"Anthony Rutledge, of course. And I know Anthony. He wouldn't. I mean he had no reason to."

"How do you know so much about Anthony?"

"Let's not play games. We both know him. Do you see Anthony jumping?"

"You tell me."

———

"Robert, my man, Joseph here. Got five hundred thou headed your way. Send it to the laundromat. All of it."

"What are you talking about? And by the way. I didn't figure you would do anything so fast. I mean, it was just a thought. And the whole business might have been coming to an end anyway. This isn't how it was supposed to go."

"Listen, and listen carefully, punk. I got a witness seen you on that roof. With Anthony Rutledge. Reliable enough to fuck you up. Now Boss Man drops five hundred thou in my lap. Says to pass it along. So, get ready for what's being delivered in cash. Fix it so we got it under wraps."

"I don't see how. What if somebody finds out?"

"Nobody's gonna find out. And we're keeping tabs on you, so just keep your fucking trap shut."

―――――

"No suicide note on the Anthony Rutledge business," said the detective. "No reason for him to do anything like this. And nobody gained from it that we can see. Why would he do it? If that's what happened. They do have a new client with possible Mafia ties. But it's all guesswork. Dead end."

―――――

"We got a call at the police station, Chief, from Robert somebody, head money guy at Rutledge's company. Wants to confess something about the Rutledge death."

"Did he say he killed him?"

"No, but seems he had something to do with it. Very confusing. Be in tomorrow morning."

―――――

Breaking News

ROBERT STIKER ... FOUND DEAD FROM FALL. SAME BUILDING HIS BOSS FELL FROM LAST MONTH.

———

"So much for Robert Stiker's confession, Chief. Where do we go from here?"

———

"Sophie? This is Carmen, Anthony Rutledge's wife—widow, that is. I know we both talked briefly at the funerals. But I think we should, you know, really talk, not on the phone, in person. Here's my address."

———

"Glad you could come over, Sophie. Have a seat. I'll get coffee. We've got a lot to discuss. And forgive me, but it's been awhile, and I think we need to move on from the grieving widow chitchat."

"Agreed."

"Okay, first of all, I was well aware of your affair with Anthony. He had a history. Then again, I know he was about to break it off. I can always tell. And this time I really thought we had a chance to, you know, start over. That's why it doesn't make any sense. I mean, why would he go and do something so awful?"

"And Robert knew about us, Carmen. He caught us in my bedroom. Came home unexpectedly, then took off as soon as he saw us. I'm sure of it. And he was pissed. And you were right. I also saw signs of an ending coming between me and Anthony."

"Guess I'm glad to have that confirmed. Small consolation. But would your Robert be mad enough to seek revenge?"

"Mad, yes. Capable of killing? No way."

"Okay, so here are the facts. Robert wouldn't have killed Anthony. And Anthony wouldn't have killed himself. Given?"

"Given."

"Same with Robert. He didn't fall off that roof by accident."

"So, who in the world? And why would anybody? And for what reason? Makes no sense."

"Okay, Nancy Drew, I'm going to say my Robert would be surprised and mad. Very mad. Not mad enough to actually kill. But mad enough to think about it. And maybe even talk about it with somebody. Then again, he had no friends. Spent all of his waking hours on his work. At the expense of our marriage, I might add."

"Is that why you took up with Anthony?"

"Maybe. Who knows how these things happen."

"This is crazy, but could your Robert have offhandedly talked with somebody about a stupid killing-for-revenge thing?"

"I don't know. I just don't know. But with no outside friends, it would have to have been company-related."

"Is this worth talking about some more with the police?"

"We both want answers."

———

"We're glad you want to continue working with the police on this investigation, ladies. Perhaps we can find leads on what has been, so far, a dead end. We're looking further into your former husbands' connections, emails, appointment books. And we'd like to spend some more time with both of you. Would you like bodyguards?"

"No. I don't think so."

"I don't either."

"I strongly advise you to take us up on our offer. Really."

———

"Listen, Boss Man, those broads have both gone back to the police. Who knows what they're blabbing about. They probably know about the money laundry stuff. Want me to do something about it?"

"You stop with your crazy fucking solutions, Joseph. It's a fucking problem that really isn't a problem. Do you enjoy tossing patsies off rooftops?"

"I fix things."

"Stop fixing. Or you'll be fixing in the pen."

"I could easily—"

"You could easily shut your trap."

"I will, Boss Man. But let me tell you one more thing could really fuck us up … they got police tails."

———

"Carmen, Sophie here. I got a call from some guy who says he's got a lead on our husbands' murders. Says he can't go to the police because he's a wanted man. They would lock him up right away. Says if he gives us a tip that works out, he might be able to do a deal with the police. Go easy on him for solving a case. Something like that."

"Sounds fishy."

"I know. Still, he said we could meet in a public place. Guaranteed safe. But we can't call the police. Said they'd arrest him and not give him a chance to explain."

"I don't like it, but: I do like the idea of playing Nancy Drew. So, I could hide with a cell phone to call for help, if needed, while you meet with him."

"Now, how do we slip our police escorts, Nancy Drew?"

"Need a plan, Sophie. Listen to this one."

"Listening."

"Both police escorts are guys. And one place guys don't normally hang out is in a beauty parlor."

"Your point?"

"My point is, we're going to a large, crowded beauty parlor. I just happen to know the owner of one. Used to be a good friend of Anthony's. She owes me. And once we're in there, we're both going to get toweled, and curled and blow-dried and moved around a lot and finally hustled out of there, sans police escorts."

"And so that's then we start playing detectives extraordinare?"

"Yes. Sophie, you set up the meeting. Outside, open. I'll have you in my sight. Lobster Shack on the water might be good."

———

"Glad you came to meet me. Don't you have a girlfriend traveling companion?"

"It's just me, Sophie. Now what information do you have about my husband's murder? You did say murder, didn't you?"

"Yeah, I did. But let's move over to that table, in the corner, by the parking lot. Away from nosy people, if you get my drift … Easier to do our business …"

"I'm not going to stay long."

"No, you're not."

"Let go of me! You're hurting me."

———

"Captain, this is Carmen. Sophie's been kidnapped, I have the license plate number."

———

"We found the car Carmen called in about. Sophie's kidnapper's car. Stolen."

———

"Boss Man, listen. It's me, Joseph."

"I can tell, and you sound fucked up. Where are you calling from?"

"Basement hideout."

"What the shit are you up to?"

"Got Sophie tied up."

"I don't believe this. What are you going to do?"

"Kill her."

"Okay Joseph, you put the phone down. Don't move a goddamn inch. Don't touch Sophie. I got the boys here and we'll be over in a sec just to check things out …"

———

"He hung up, good. Listen boys, we got a job to do. Kill that fucking idiot. Can't have him around anymore. I thought he might pull some stupid shit like this."

———

"Guess we're fucked now, Boss Man. She's seen him. And that will tie the whole business to our company."

"Pay attention, we haven't done a thing. We can distance ourselves from Joseph. It'll all be on that bonehead, that dead bonehead. So, we're going to turn her loose, without her seeing anybody else. Then we're going to set up a meeting with both girls at my office. Play dumb. Ask questions. They're smart, see what's on their minds."

———

"Nancy Drew was never as lucky as you, Sophie. You think we should get out of the detective business?"

"I don't know. But I just got a call from my late husband's newest client. They want to talk."

Breaking News

MALE, ID JOSEPH MARVO ... FOUND DEAD FROM FALL SAME BUILDING AS TWO OTHER MEN FELL FROM

"Sophie, this is the Police Chief calling."

"Yes, Chief."

"Have you seen today's paper?"

"I have."

"Did you see the picture of the man who fell from the same building your husband fell from?"

"Yes."

"Do you recognize him?"

"No, should I?"

"Well, he worked for a company that does business for the company where your husband Robert worked."

"That is strange. Is there a connection?"

"We don't know. But if you think of anything to connect the events, we would certainly appreciate a call. Oh, by the way, I just remembered: Let me congratulate you and Carmen on the purchase of that company, what with both of you losing your husbands."

"Thank you, Chief."

———

"OK Sophie, you can be CEO for a year, then I'll take the title. Back and forth."

"Well, Carmen, I think co-CEO titles will work out just fine. We work pretty well together, don't you think?"

CHAPTER 14

DEAD WEIGHT OF
BOOTS, SKIS AND BIKES

Focusing on the three groups of freshly purchased items at his feet, Jacques considered the one-time uses he had in mind for each group: Plan A, plus two backups. Two pairs of L.L.Bean mountain climbing boots, two sets of Head skis, and two ten-speed Schwinn bikes, one male, one female.

How appropriate, he thought, *that I should be sitting in the middle of their dark, dirty garage with these brand-new, unused things.* Calling it a garage was a joke—not enough room for a car. Over the years, he'd kept moving in more and more stuff, stuff his lovely wife insisted he purchase and then nagged him to put to good use around the house. Nag, nag, nag. And now, after all that time and harassment, he is left with this: a mountain of dust-caked crap fencing him in. Items that, truth be known, he had no intention of putting to use, good, bad, or any other for that matter. Did she actually expect him to press into service any one of those goddamn rakes or hammers or shovels or saws or whatever other rusted piece of tool shit that was lying around here? She still thinks he should be her personal handyman. He didn't think so. He smiled at what he had in mind for this new equipment.

———

"I can't believe it! Patrick and Melissa separated." Wide-eyed bewilderment stretched his wife's deeply tanned, gaunt features. "Weren't you surprised? I mean they were the perfect couple, weren't they? And after twenty-five years. Didn't you think they were … perfect?"

"You know, Andrea," said Jacques, "I'm not exactly sure what you mean by perfect. I mean, twenty-five years is a long time to stick it out." His haggard tones matched his looks and feelings. "Don't you think that after such a long time … whatever?"

"And just what do you mean by 'a long time' … and 'whatever'? We're going on twenty-five years. Are you saying you're going to dump me next year?"

"Dear, you're missing my point."

"Which would be what, Dr. Phil? And what would you do with yourself, anyway? Where would you go? How would you manage all by yourself? Do you think the company would keep you on as VP? Or anything else, for that matter. Do I have to spell out how many times I've saved your ass, over the years, with our board?"

"Oh please, please. I didn't say anything about leaving you or the damn company. You're the one who brought it up. And why, for God's sake, do you always have to hammer home that it's your family's company every time we get into an argument?"

"Do I?"

"Look, can we just get off this topic? How did it go at the studio today?"

"I'm just finishing up a few mobiles. I'm going to exhibit at that Peace Corps charity show next month. I hope you'll be able to come this time. As the head of marketing, you'd think you'd be able to coordinate your time so you could attend certain events that are important to certain people. I could look at your time reports, to see how they measure up, if you like. Your paperwork is always such a mess."

"If you think I'm not doing my job, why don't you just bring it up at the next board meeting?"

"Honey, honey, that's not what I mean at all. Let's forget about this whole subject. Whatever it is. I mean, I just don't know what we were arguing about in the first place. We need to go out and have a special dinner … someplace we both like, and then take in a show. Or just come home and have a nice romantic evening. What do you say to that, dear?"

"I say that's a terrific idea. Just terrific."

<hr>

And a grand night it was. Although he was somewhat distracted, contemplating his next move.

"Dear, you didn't seem to be all there last night. Not that I didn't have a real nice time. But afterward, wasn't that very special?"

"It certainly was special. Very special, dear."

"We should do more stuff together like we used to. Remember when we did more, you know, stuff together?"

We did stuff together, he thought, *good stuff. And then we didn't anymore. Instead it was things like, "Dear, here's a list of people you need to schmooze with at tomorrow's corporate lunch. I know you'll do fine. But please avoid the political stuff you tend to bring up." Not to mention a bunch of stupid, pushy shit: "Honey, I'd skip that dessert, you're gaining a touch ..." And, "Dear, you might want to check out a health club, you're getting a little, well ...."*

"I'll think of something. Maybe after your show. And I will be going to that show, my love."

"Thank you, my little sweetie, I appreciate it. I really do."

———

"Boy, your exhibit was some smash. You must have raised a bundle for the Peace Camp."

"Peace Corps, dear, Peace Corps. But yes, I did raise quite a lot, thank you."

"That's good. Very good. Listen, remember before the show, when we talked about going off somewhere, like in the old days? You know, just the two of us?"

"Sure, but we can't be away too long. My next show's coming right up."

"Yeah, yeah, I know. I'm just talking about a brief outing. Maybe an overnight somewhere. Someplace where we can go and do something as a couple, like mountain climbing."

"Oh dear, I haven't gone mountain climbing in years. What could I wear? Don't you need special boots?"

"I'll take care of it. For both of us. All you'll need will be some old clothes—jeans, a T-shirt, comfortable things. What do you say?"

"OK, I guess. And you're going to arrange the whole thing? This is so unlike you. Have you turned over a new leaf, dear?"

"You could say that."

———

"OK love, time to get up," he urged at four in the morning. "Today's the day."

"What are you talking about?"

"Mountain climbing. Today's the day we both agreed we'd go mountain climbing. Remember?"

"Kind of. But I'm not really ready. I need clothes. And mountain climbing boots. What about that? I'm sure you need—,"

"Looky here."

"Oh my God. Are those brand new? L.L.Bean?"

"Yes, for you. And here are mine ... we'll match. Let's put them on and get out of here."

"So what else? I'll need a bit more that just boots."

"Jeans and a tee will do fine. And I put some stuff in the car for an overnight."

"What's got into you? Why, you're something else."

———

"I'm all tuckered out," she whined. "And do we need to go up so high? It doesn't look safe. Let's go back to the parking lot and find a good motel and somewhere for a nice dinner. I'm so hungry I could eat a horse."

"Only a little farther, dear, and we'll get a beautiful view. Just beautiful."

"I'm not taking one more step up. Not one more. Only down. Down to a soft bed and a nice meal."

"You'll be sorry."

"No, I won't. And hey, look down there. That couple's headed down, not up. Let's check with them. Make sure we're headed in the right direction."

"Where? I don't see anybody. Anyway, I think we should go our own way. I know where we are."

"I'm not so sure of that. I'm going down to catch them. I don't care what you do, Mr. Know-It-All Camper."

"Fine, fine, go and spoil the trip I carefully planned for you. Whatever you say."

"I say, I want to go home."

———

"You don't have to be such a grumpy grumpy, Mr. Grumpy. What is it? You're mad because we're home, and you sprained your ankle running after me. And I got my picture in the paper for saving that couple I spotted on the mountain? Well, didn't the paper make a big deal of it? I mean they were both lost and frightened, she was dehydrated, I gave her water and we all found our way back. So I didn't actually save them, but they went and put my picture on the front page. Must have been a slow news day, ha, ha. I still don't understand why you were in such a hurry to follow me down. Dear ... now why are you so quiet? Is it because they didn't mention you in the article? Why don't you tell me what you're thinking?"

I'm thinking, he considered, *that this whole stupid scenario reminds me of one of her company's board meetings where she's in the spotlight and I'm a lost turd in the background.*

"I'm thinking I need a rest."

"Of course you do."

But then, she considered, *why did he run after me like that? He seemed almost frantic in an effort to get me to do something. What, I can't say for sure. Wasn't that just like him to head off in some silly direction without any thought as to where he was going?*

"Anyway, no need for a snit, love. Is your ankle feeling better yet? Let me see it."

"Don't touch it. I mean, there's no need, it's fine, just fine. Why don't you check on the health of the couple you saved from death's door?"

"Let's forget about that couple and think about us."

"Yes, and you know what comes to my mind? A comfy lodge, a wood fire, hot toddies and the warm glow of accomplishing, oh ... one thing or another. I'll get back to you."

———

"OK sweetheart. Remember when we used to ski in Colorado? Well, I was thinking to bring back those old memories."

"I haven't been on skis in years. I'm not sure I even remember how to put them on."

"I'll take care of everything. Trust me."

It was five a.m. And he gently shook her. "Time to get up, honey bunny. The Ski Vail Special leaves the airport in two hours, remember?"

"Kind of. Are you sure today's the day?"

"It is. And we're all packed and ready to head for the slopes and a brand new chapter in our marriage."

"It's late, I'm freezing, and it's been an awfully long day. Can we head for the lodge now?"

"One more run, love. Aren't you having a good time?"

"Yes, of course. But look at the time."

"One last run to the top."

"I don't recognize this trail, and it seems so … empty. Do you know where we are?"

"Yes, I do know. Let's start down over there. I'll follow and watch how you're doing."

"And my skis seem loose. Are you sure you checked them carefully at the lift back there?"

"I did and they're just fine. Now point them down and I'll be right here to make sure you're OK."

I don't know, she reflected, as she furtively reached down and quickly tightened the skis she knew were loose.

———

"Doctor, how's he doing? He's such a good skier, but then he made this funny move reaching for me. To help me, I guess, because you see there was this tree in my way. Like it came up from nowhere. And if I hadn't tripped on a bump, I would have … I don't know. So instead, Jacques sails over me and slams off the tree—oh dear, I just can't talk about it anymore. It's so … so terrible. What I mean is, how is he? Is he going to be all right?"

"He'll live, thanks to your grabbing his leg before he went over the edge and certain death. The nurse brought him this morning's paper. Nice picture of you on the front page. You seem to be a lifesaving hero. A couple in distress and now your husband. I'm sure he'll enjoy reading about you. Take his mind off his current condition."

———

Surrounded by all the junk in the garage, sitting in the wheelchair he would be confined to for the rest of his life, he eyeballed the only remaining item of the shiny new equipment he'd started out with: one male ten-speed Schwinn bike. She was out on hers, engaging in her new-found passion. "I feel just awful," she had said, "with you being so confined and all. But it was really thoughtful of you to buy these bikes for us in the first place. And I can't believe how much I love cycling, all thanks to you and your healthy lifestyle encouragements. It was like, after all those years of inactivity, I saw the light, the minute I found the bikes."

"I bought them for us—I can't join you, but no matter—I can still enjoy you enjoying yourself."

"Now don't brood over me … it wasn't your fault. It was just one of those things. We'll have the rest of our lives together to make the best of what we do have."

"The best of whatever fucking garbage this shit-hole life deals us," he spat out to himself, as she turned left out of the driveway.

———

He wheeled himself into the company lawyer's office just as they started reading her will, a week after she was blindsided by a drunk driver on one of her many bike outings.

"Now, Jacques," said one of the company lawyers Jacques had never seen before, "no reason for you to stay for the full reading of this rather lengthy document. You need only concern yourself with this diary, the one on the table. Andrea started keeping it shortly after your unfortunate skiing accident. Basically, after thinking things through, and piecing together certain bits of information—evidence, if you will—Andrea came to the conclusion that you had tried to harm her then."

"I—" blurted out Jacques. "That is, how can I answer that?"

"There's no need to," the lawyer broke in. "It's not a question. And you're not on trial here. That's what she thought. And that's that. So here's the only part of her will that involves you. It's ironic, because she expressed some concern that you might try something else along those nefarious lines. But no, not to worry about that now, no one's accusing you of any involvement in the bike accident. No one. So anyway, more to the point, having been duly appointed trustee, I will hereby commence reading that portion of her will that pertains to you, Jacques."

The lawyer peered over his reading glasses at the will. "I bequeath to my husband two almost-new L.L.Bean hiking boots, two sets of barely used Head skis, and two Schwinn ten-speeds."

"As appointed trustee, I hereby amend this will to read one Schwinn ten-speed. And that's all she wrote."

CHAPTER 15

A Peeping Tom Spies a Dead End

"Got time for a quick one, before we shove off for home and face our better halves?"

"Don't I always?"

"There must have been a time when we skipped it. But for the life of me, I can't remember when."

"Don't forget to hand in your time sheet. What a pain. Not like the good ole days when we just showed up for work and did our job. And you're the one who fucked things up."

"What did I do?"

"You know damn well. You're the techie genius who introduced our new, fancy-dancy electronic time sheets and installed that shit-ass automatic camera system. It's like we're being stalked 24–7. Can't get away with anything."

"Sorry about that. But you must admit, it's much easier to keep track of things around here now."

"I'll give you that. But I kind of miss the old-fashioned way of doing business."

"I understand what you mean. My counter: Get over it."

"Still say you fucked things up."

———

"Cheers: See you're going for the hard stuff this afternoon, a double, no less. Moving up from your regular Bud Light to something a little more serious. Everything all right?"

"Fine, just fine. Feel a little stressed is all. Not really sure why. Same office bullshit we've both faced all these years, I guess."

"And we've been at it for a while, tried and true."

"We have."

"You sure there's nothing serious stuck in your craw? Nothing you'd like to share with a buddy? Wouldn't be the first time we've hashed out little difficulties in our worthless lives."

"You're right. And thanks. But I'm fine."

"Good. Oh by the way, you know Gladys Finley?"

"Not sure. Could be, why?"

"Well, she's in accounting and seems she reported seeing a Peeping Tom from her bedroom window. Happened before, she said. The police were around the other day. They talk to you?"

"Guess they did, briefly. Come to think of it. Her picture looked vaguely familiar. I said her name didn't ring a bell."

"Isn't it disgusting the way our society is headed? I don't remember that kind of stuff going on when we were young."

"Probably was. We just weren't paying any attention."

"Maybe. So what do you think goes through the sick mind of somebody like that?"

"Don't know."

"Well, what do you think?"

"Haven't given it much thought."

"Want to know what I think? I think he's fucked up. Probably got a shitty home life. Wife doesn't put out. Can't keep a job. Old lady supports him. Hangs out around kids' playgrounds. Maybe he's gay. Or partly gay. Could go both ways, that kind of stuff. Any ideas?"

"You seem to have them all. Where'd you get that profile?"

"Where'd I get it? Don't know. It's just what comes to mind when I think about it. How about you?"

"How about me? Don't really have an opinion. I suppose it's been going on for a while. And, I don't know why … I just don't know."

"Okay, unlike you to not have an opinion. But whatever."

———

"Down the hatch. Here's to the life we should have had."

"I'll drink to that."

"When did we start our have-a-quick-one before our heading home from the office habit?"

"When was the last time we missed one?"

"Think it was before the ice age."

"No, it was before the big bang."

"Always have to have the last word, don't you?"

"Listen, on a serious note: Do you know Ronda Rodinsky?"

"Not sure, why?"

"Anyway, she's in production, and word is she found this camera, this tiny electronic device, in her shower. It's only because her boyfriend's a techie that it was discovered."

"Guess a girl can't be too careful."

"I mean, how would somebody do something like that? And would that person be able to see everything in the shower? But it was found. Wouldn't it be easy to find?"

"A slip-up."

"What?"

"Nothing. Maybe somebody didn't know what he, or she, was doing, I guess."

———

"I'm really sorry to bother you with a phone call at the office," she apologized. "You free for a minute?"

"I've got some spare time. What's up?"

"This is really embarrassing. And I apologize in advance for putting you in the middle of a situation."

"Middle of what? What are you talking about?"

"Thing is, I just don't know what to do. And you two have been such close office buddies for so long."

"We have. Please tell me what's on your mind."

"I'm so confused … But it's like this. I would like you to talk to my husband about something."

"I don't understand."

"It's, it's … well, it's stuff I've found of his. Like pictures. See, I was searching through his personal things—I know, I know, I'm not supposed to be doing anything like that. But after all the recent publicity about that camera. That camera found in that girl's shower. Well, I've had suspicions. And I just started looking around. And the thing is … see, I found these things, things I just can't talk to him about … I really can't. Can you? … Can you say something to him? … and find out if it all means anything?"

"I don't know what to say … I mean, I guess so."

———

"Drinks on me this afternoon, buddy."

"Hey, we always pay for our own. You know that."

"This is different. Order up. And you might want to make yours a double."

"What the dickens are you talking about?"

"Take a swig, relax and listen to me. Now, don't take this the wrong way, my friend, but I've got to tell you something. Something kind of personal. Because, you see, out of nowhere, your wife called me here at the office."

"Called you? What for?"

"Yeah, I was taken aback. But I had some spare time. And I listened to her. Said she found some things of yours. She didn't know who to talk to about it. Said it sounds so stupid but she's just too embarrassed to talk to you. Knows we've been best bros forever, of course, and she was at her wits' end. Told me stuff she found included some tiny electronic device in his—that would be your, clothes."

"What in the world was she doing?"

"Right. Said she knew snooping was not good. But she read in the paper about what they found in that girl's shower. And, she said, 'I can't imagine that my husband would do anything like that …' But there've been other items she said she found. Said she just couldn't bring herself to talk about it with you, just couldn't. And she knew it was scatterbrained and all, but asked me to talk to you. She understands it's awful to put me in the middle, but knows how close we are. And then asked me if I thought she should just shut up and forget it. Or what? So, should she just shut up and forget it?"

"I don't know what to say. We've known each other nonstop, forever, haven't we?"

"Yeah, so?"

"See, it's like this. There's always something you don't know about a close friend. Cause you think you know everything. But you never do."

"Are you saying your wife's right? That you're one of those Peeping Toms? How could that be?"

"I know. That sounds so gross. But I guess there are worse things."

"I suppose. But thing is, what are you going to do about it? How about counseling? What do you say?"

"Maybe, but I'd like to try to work this out myself. I'll tell her we talked. Not the first time we've worked out things between us … I'll try to make her understand."

"It's a start."

"And listen, I'm so sorry you got caught in the middle. I know it's not fair. Why should you have to go through all this shit, just because we're … well, I'm so sorry."

"Don't be. Just keep me informed. I'm here for you, as always."

"So, are you going to say anything to the police?"

"No, of course not. No real harm's been done. We—or that is, you—will just straighten this whole thing out. And put an end to it all. Will you promise me that?"

"Yeah, yeah, I'll start. I promise. Oh, you remember that electric razor I borrowed from you ages ago?"

"I think so, but didn't you say you left it in a hotel room? Forget it."

"No. I've got a new one. I'll leave yours in your locker. Got the combination, as you know."

"No need."

"No, really, I'll just drop it off."

"Okay, if you insist."

"I do."

———

Local Female Executive, MISSING FOR DAYS
FOUND BLUDGEONED TO DEATH IN HER APARTMENT

———

"Did you see the morning paper?"

"Glanced at it. Why?"

"Why? One of our own employees was killed. That's why. What the hell is going on here? A Peeping Tom. Camera in a shower. And now this. What do you know about this?"

"Listen, yes, I confess I've been guilty of some Peeping Tom stuff. But I am not a killer. Go to the police, if you must. But please believe me: I would never even think of doing anything so, so horrible. God's truth."

"How can I be sure?"

"Go to the police, if you must. Understand, if you do, I'll be in a lot of trouble. I know it looks bad. But believe me, really: I'm innocent."

"OK, OK. Let's hope they find this guy soon."

———

"Drink up. And make it a good one."

"It's always good."

"I know, but this is different."

"What's up?"

"See, the police came to me yesterday, out of the blue. And wanted to search my locker. They asked did I mind? They had a search warrant anyway. I said OK. And shit … guess what?"

"What?"

"First of all, the whole thing with the cops was based on an anonymous tip. And they found squat in my locker, except for that razor, the one you returned, remember? And, a screwdriver. What's that all about? It's not my screwdriver. Did you put something in my locker along with the stupid razor you went on about? What's going on here?"

"Don't know. Can't talk."

———

"She was killed around noon, Sergeant. Went home unexpectedly, sick. Several days later she was found dead. Appears as though she must have surprised somebody, like an intruder. Looks like a scuffle ensued. Forensics concluded she was stabbed, but not with a household knife. They're thinking some kind of blunt instrument, judged to be a device resembling a screwdriver."

"So, what would an intruder be doing with a screwdriver? More like a workman than an intruder. And now an anonymous tip leads us to a screwdriver in this guy's locker. Yes, her blood was on it. No prints. Stashed away and all, but why wouldn't he have thrown it away?"

"No time to find a good hiding spot?"

"Could be. And we think it was somebody in her office. The Peeping Tom incidence and the camera found in the bathroom. All point to that office."

"Alibis?"

"Regular busy, workday activities. We're checking on everybody. Hard to pin down exact times. Nothing so far."

———

"Now, where do we stand?"

"OK. We have two guys here. Guy with screwdriver in his locker is pointing the finger at an old buddy of his as a Peeping Tom. Buddy is claiming innocence. Double-checking both stories. Office schedules not easy to verify."

"Talk to their wives?"

"Finger-pointer's wife backs up what he told us. So what?"

"Go on."

"First there's finger-pointer guy, also known as screwdriver-in-his-locker guy. Screwdriver matches the wounds on the victim. And it's her blood on the screwdriver. But no prints."

"It's his locker. Wouldn't he wipe them off?"

"Of course. But why not the blood?"

"Hard to get rid of it all."

"Maybe. And screwdriver guy claims his buddy confessed to him that he was a Peeping Tom, after he got a call from Peeping Tom's wife."

"And what does alleged Peeping Tom say?"

"Denies it."

"And alleged Peeping Tom's wife?"

"Clams up."

"Unless we can verify the finger-pointer's buddy as a Peeping Tom, he's in the clear. And his wife is not about to help us."

"So we're looking at screwdriver-in-locker guy? That would be the finger pointer?"

"Yeah."

———

"We can't stay here. I'm a marked man, even without a trial. Will you come with me?"

"Where? Where in the world are we going?"

"I don't know. Maybe Canada or Mexico. I haven't been convicted or even charged with anything. We can start a new life. And we both know you have faith in me. I mean, you haven't said anything to the police. We're a team."

"I guess we are. I'm so mixed up about what took place. Of course I sort of know what took place. But what really happened?"

"What happened? Okay, you know I'm guilty of something. And you haven't said a thing. Thank you. So I owe you an explanation. Yes, I was there doing whatever when she shows up, just like that. There she is. She goes crazy. She recognizes me, of course. And starts screaming my name. And yelling stuff like you're the fucking Peeping Tom, aren't you? You fucker. And she starts pounding on me. I try to block her, But she keeps at it. Harder. So I just took the thing I was holding, the screwdriver, and went to hold her back and she got stabbed. I mean, it was an accident. Really. But then she was bleeding. And I didn't know what to do. She saw me. And I just did the only thing I could."

"Oh, my God. You did kill her. I kind of thought so all along."

"It was an accident, can't you see that?"

"I'm trying to make sense of it all."

"Here's the phone. Call the police. Go ahead. I'll probably spend the rest of my life in prison. For a ... a misfortune ... a freak incident. I certainly didn't mean to ... well, you know."

"I don't know. How can we start fresh with this hanging over our heads?"

"I haven't been charged. We can make a clean break with the past. Really, I promise to get rid of ... of any bad habits."

"Promise?"

"Promise. We can go to Mexico. Where nobody knows us. Just the two of us. A fresh start."

Man With The Blood-Stained
Screwdriver In His Locker Is
CHARGED WITH MURDER

"As your lawyer, I need something definite, for the trial, as to your whereabouts at the time of death."

"We've been over this. I'm doing the best I can. I was all over the place. I can't pinpoint a time or provide a witness for the jury."

"Just tell me the truth. And acting as your legal counsel, I should be able to keep you out of court. Unlike your buddy. Now, you were watching a training film at the time of death. Is that right?"

"Yes."

"In the dark?"

"Well, yes."

———

"My lawyer says I'll probably never be charged."

"What if you just tell the police it was an accident? Get your buddy off the hook."

"Should I? And spend the rest of my life in prison? Why don't we wait and see how the trial comes out. He'll probably get off. And that will be that."

Screwdriver Killer
SENTENCED TO THIRTY YEARS

"I hate Mexico. We can never go back, can we?"

POLICE BLOTTER

New DNA trace on "screwdriver" case reveals unidentified additional suspect.

Murder verdict reversed. Case unsolved.

George Is Missing

"Well, it's good to see you again after all this time. Come into my abode. Let me show you to my favorite chair. It's the least I can do for a long-lost buddy."

"Good to see you, too. How long? Fifteen, twenty years?"

"More like twenty-five, my man. Time flies. But I'm glad you looked me up. So what brings you here, back to your roots? Miss me?"

"Yeah. Actually, just happen to be passing through. And, as you can see, still remember your old address."

"That's a good thing. Now the last time I saw you, was … was right before you left town, if I'm not mistaken. After that trip you and George took. So, did they ever find George? I lost track."

"No, sorry to say, they didn't."

"No leads? No idea what the dickens could have happened to him? I mean, how did it end up? It was a big news story for a while. Then nothing. My sister Mary Anne—your former fiancée, remember?—finally left town. And nobody seemed to know anything. Did you spend much time with the police?"

"What do you mean by that?"

"Nothing. I'm just wondering. Aren't you still wondering? Because it was all so strange. Just went missing. And nothing. No clues that we knew of."

"What can I say? That's not what I came here to talk about. What about your family? Still married to Millie? Any kids? I mean, I'm totally out of the loop about what's happened here. You finish law school?"

"I finished. I have two boys. Twins. Both are launched. Both married. They own a restaurant with their spouses in Denver. Which they started while ski bumming around Vail. So you don't know that Millie died of cancer a couple of years ago? I visit the kids on a regular basis."

"Sorry. Always liked Millie. So you're a lawyer? Very impressed."

"Small town legal beagle. That's me in a nutshell. Now give me your story. And I'm sorry, but you've got to tell me more about what might have happened to George."

"Nothing to tell."

"Oh come on, you looked me up. I showed you mine. Your turn."

"So … divorced. Three marriages. Between jobs. On my way to visit an old girlfriend. Possible opening in her real estate company. Couldn't resist looking you up. And have no idea what happened to George."

"Okey dokey. Well, I happen to be a criminal lawyer. Mind if I put on my legal beagle hat?"

"Listen. This is old stuff."

"Please. Just enough to satisfy my curiosity. Morbid curiosity, if you will."

"Make it short. Got to go. Early plane to catch."

"Right, but tell me about when you last saw George. What he said. Exactly what he said. That's a question I would ask if I were on the case. What the heck did you and George talk about?"

"That's what the police asked me. Said I wasn't sure."

"Not sure? Just the two of you on this fishing holiday, and you can't remember what you guys talked about?"

"Talked the usual bullshit. Planned to get up at four to go fishing. Same ole, same ole."

"And?"

"And he wasn't there the next morning."

"You didn't hear anything?"

"Nothing."

"How about his stuff?"

"All there."

"His clothes?"

"Nothing touched."

"Bed?"

"Slept in. But he was gone."

"Didn't the police find anything? Nothing that could help them with what might have happened?"

"Nothing. And they looked. Believe me."

"And you left town right after. Where'd you go? Nobody seemed to know."

"I went west. Nothing to stick around for."

"Where?"

"San Francisco. It's funny, because I considered heading to Vail, become a ski bum. But thought better of it."

"You might have run across my boys. But why did you leave so quickly? Nobody had any idea where you went. Mary Anne and I were both mystified. She finally got married, by the way. She kept hoping you would get in touch. But you never did."

"Yeah. No point."

"Not even a call or a note? She was devastated. I mean, why?"

"Had nothing to say. It was all over."

"What do you mean by that? You were set to make it official. I know you two had plans and everything."

"Right. But then George said something and … never mind, got to go."

"Wait a minute here. You can't just go and leave me out on a limb like that. Finish your story. I saw there was an investigation. Paper said you were cleared. But it was out of the news so fast. Hush, hush, and before anybody knew anything, you were gone. What's with that?"

"Nothing's with that. I really gotta get going. Don't know what got into me. Think I made a mistake coming here."

"Fine. You go wherever. But I got to tell you something been on my mind for a long time. You see, as a lawyer, I was curious and I looked for the records on that investigation … Missing."

"I know."

"What do you mean, you know?"

"I mean, it's been a long time. Records go missing."

"No. I looked for them right after you left."

"Your point?"

"My point is, what happened to them? Somebody must have taken them. And how did you know they were gone?"

"Just assumed."

"I think you're lying. I can tell. I'm a lawyer. A lawyer who smells something fishy."

"So what? Who cares what you think you know?"

"You might care. After I tell you this weird story from the past. Here's the thing: Some time after you left town so abruptly, Mary Anne called me and asked if she could meet me at my house. I was married by then and in law school. So Mary Anne comes over and tells me she's tired of waiting. And she's met this nice man and is planning on getting married. She told me that she loves this nice man and all … 'But to be honest,' she says, 'because you are my brother, I have to tell you: I can't forget him,' meaning you, that is. And then Sis goes and opens up this grocery bag she had with her and pulls out a dirty old hunting shirt. 'It's his,' she said, 'the one he wore on his last trip with George. I snuck it from the house. And kept it. Never washed it. Not sure why. But it smells like him. He was acting weird after that trip. I had this feeling he was going to leave me. He looked at me funny. Like he was mad at something. Maybe something dumb I may have done and regretted. Whatever. I know I'm acting like a silly little schoolgirl with a crush … But I'm getting married and so I can't keep it any longer. I know this is stupid and all, and I know he's never coming back—but can you keep it? Lawyers do stuff like that, don't they? Am I making any sense? You're my brother, but let me pay you to take care of this.'

"I told her I wasn't a lawyer, yet. But that didn't matter. And yes, I could certainly keep it. At no charge, of course. 'Because,' I said, 'you're my first client. Of a not-yet lawyer.'"

"What in the world is the point to that ridiculous shaggy-dog nonsense story?"

"The point is I still have that shirt. Never did anything with it. Felt kind of sorry for Mary Anne. And I kept it. Thinking that … oh, I don't know what. But of course we still keep in touch."

"So what d'ya want me to do?"

"Nothing. I'm just curious about what I might find if I had an analysis done, see if there's anything on your shirt."

"It's got my DNA. So what?"

"So your DNA is a given. As a criminal lawyer I'd look for things like somebody else's DNA."

"So what if you did find George's DNA? You don't even know when I wore that shirt."

"Okay, if I was the prosecuting attorney I wouldn't care exactly when you wore the shirt. I'd be more interested about what's on the shirt. So, I'm picturing myself in front of a jury. First I'd hold up the evidence receptacle containing the grocery bag with your shirt. Hand it over to the sheriff with a flourish. Then take out a color photo of the shirt and pass it around to the jury."

"What's the point in doing all that?"

"The point is to create some drama. Get their attention."

"And what are you going to say when you've got their attention?"

"Do and say. First I would make a show of looking for an envelope, then find it and haul out a large assemblage of forensic papers. I would read portions of these papers to the jury. Details of what was found on the shirt. I'd be looking for … oh, I don't know … bloodstains. Skin fragments, whatever. See, I wouldn't need George to convict. Parts of him would do just fine for my case."

"Okay. Give you a thousand."

"What?"

"Make it two."

"What the heck are you saying?"

"I'm saying, let's move on from a bad situation. One I've had to live with all these years."

"Tell me."

"Shit. It was an accident. He fucked Mary Anne. He told me. And laughed about it. Big fucking joke. We got into a fight. Hit his head on the mantel. Dead. I guess.

If not, I finished the fucker off. If you want to know the truth. But not my fault."

"What happened to the body?"

"Logging camp with a wood chipper. Took it to a landfill, up north, long deserted. Been going to this camp for years. Know all about the area."

"Why are you telling me this? Is this why you came back after all this time?"

"Really don't know. Feel guilty, I guess. Even though it was an accident, as I see it. I mean, we did fight. But I certainly didn't plan on killing him. And I feel badly about Mary Anne. I couldn't go back to her. But you and Mary Ann have always been on my mind. And I figured I was free and clear by now. No matter what I happened to say to you. But now that stupid hunting shirt pops up. I mean, there's probably nothing on it that would make any difference. But I'd like to get rid of it. Peace of mind, you understand."

"Oh, I understand all right. And I haven't touched it since I tucked it away. I keep it in the … never mind where."

"Not going to search your house now or sneak back in the night. But …"

"But you'd like to get hold of that shirt and, and what? Destroy it?"

"I guess. No statute of limitations on murder, if that's what it was. Right?"

"Whatever. But I have no desire to resurrect this matter. I do, however, believe your conscience is getting to you."

"I've pretty much fucked up my whole life. Even now. On my way to beg an old, crazy-ass girlfriend for a bullshit job. Story of my useless life. Guess I felt the need to talk about it, to somebody—whoever. It's a weight on my shoulders the size of a … well, the size of a landfill. Now isn't that ironic? Know where Mary Anne is? Has kids and everything I assume."

"I do know where she is. And yes. Two kids. Twin girls. Runs in the family. We have a nice long phone chat every year. Always asks me if I still have that shirt."

"You're not going to sell me that shirt, are you?"

"No."

"Well, fuck it. I'm out of here. You do whatever you want with the shirt. Here's my address, if you want to charge me. But it'll change soon. Always does."

————

"Hello, Mary Anne? Why don't you take a break, a couple of days off, and come down for a visit. I've got a story to tell you and it needs to be told in person."

CHAPTER 17

CRACKED
EASTER EGG HUNT

"**N**ow be a good little boy and stop that. No, you cannot kick that little girl in the leg and take her Easter egg just because you can't find one for yourself. Oh my God, I think she's bleeding. What's going on here? Ouch! Hey, good little boys don't kick their teachers, either. Now you stop that or I'm going to … What the dickens am I going to do here? And now you? I don't need another little person to help me out here, so you can just let go of that other little boy, the one you think is doing something bad to me, I guess … Anyway, I can take care of the situation all by myself, thank you very much. Now my little miss, how is that leg of yours? Ouch! Wait a second here, why in the world are you kicking me? You found your own Easter egg, didn't you? What's your goddamn problem? Yes, yes, I know, I said a bad word.

And I'm really sorry, but it's just that I—Now hold your horses, all you little boys and girls. Hey! Way over there, yes, in the corner, you can't be doing that. I mean you just can't. Oh please, please dear God, tell me this isn't all happening to me."

"Okay Mr. La Chase, can you tell us exactly what happened at the Happy Day Nursery School this morning?"

"Of course, Officer. The thing is, I was asked—at the last minute, I might add—to supervise the annual Happy Day Nursery School Easter Egg Hunt, all by myself, some kind of last-minute emergency staff meeting, they said. Since I'm new here, my presence at the meeting was not exactly critical. So I was available. The point is, I couldn't say no, but I didn't know the kids all that well. I mean, they didn't even tell me where the eggs were hidden, for gosh sake. Last minute, as I mentioned."

"Yes, yes, you told us. But we need to understand precisely what took place."

"Yeah, well it's kind of confusing. Listen, why all the questions? And why are the police involved anyway?"

"Precisely what took place?"

"All of a sudden I was, you see, in kind of a messy situation. Well, you know, I was doing all right at first. The kids were having a good time. A great time. But then this little boy kind of kicked this little girl. I didn't see it at first. I was, oh, doing something else to help the kids, naturally. Anyway, this little boy was upset because he couldn't find an egg, and she had an egg. So he went right up to this girl and took aim. It was just awful; I saw blood, but what could I do? And then another little guy grabbed the kicker, to help her, the one bleeding, I guess, but I told him no. And then she—the kicked little girl, that is—well, she goes and she kicks me. She had her Easter egg, so she had no good reason to. But there you are, it was kind of like all hell, all of a sudden, sort of broke loose. I mean to say the kids were all over the place, kicking and screaming. 'Cause they're kids, you understand. And I was just trying to reason with them. But I'm new here and I don't really know …"

"Of course. Now please just tell us what went on after, as best as you can remember."

"Well then, this teacher, out of the blue, who I don't know from Adam, mind you, comes up to me and says that everything would be taken care of, told me I should leave. And I said I didn't think it was such a great idea. 'Just look around,' I said. And that's when I was told, in no uncertain terms, to leave. More or less ordered out."

"And just who was this teacher?"

"I told you, I don't know. Never seen him before."

"Then how do you know this teacher was actually a teacher?"

"Yeah, well, I guess I don't actually know. But that's what it looked like."

"So tell us, did you see any serious injuries?"

"I already told you, I saw the one little girl's leg was bleeding. The one who was kicked."

"Anything more serious?"

"Well, no. Exactly what do you mean by serious? I'm sure she'll be all right. I think she'll live."

"Here's the thing. We have a deceased student on our hands."

"For Christ's sake, who? No. That's not possible. There must be some mistake. Because when I left, things seemed to be getting better. That teacher said not to worry. And sure, the one little girl was bleeding and all that. And I didn't take a real close look. But I can't imagine."

"Now, Mr. La Chase, this is a possible homicide investigation."

"No. I don't believe it. What're you saying? That I'm a suspect in some kind of murder case?"

"We're not saying anything of the kind. We're simply conducting an investigation into a death. We don't know the circumstances. We have a few more questions for you."

"Who died? Was it that little girl? I don't even know her name. What was her name, anyway?"

"We'll ask the questions, if you don't mind. Now, did this alleged teacher give you a name?"

"No."

"Then can you give us a description? Male or female?"

"Well now, this is weird. Because I'm not really sure if I was looking at a man or a woman."

"Are you saying you can't tell us if this person, the one who requested that you leave a very nasty situation, was male or female?"

"First of all, I don't think I used the word nasty. Serious perhaps. But I can tell you, from my experience as an educator, kids will be kids. And this teacher assured me everything would be hunky-dory."

"Alleged teacher."

"Who am I to question? I already told you, I'm new here and so how do you expect me to know?"

"We don't expect anything. We're only trying to get all the facts straight."

"Get the facts from him."

"Are you saying you think the teacher was male?"

"It's just an expression. Male, female, I have no idea."

"How would you describe this person?"

"Listen, have you ever been in a room full of out-of-control kids, I mean really out of control? What I'm saying is that everything was fine until, oh, I don't know, until everything wasn't fine. I really can't remember much of anything. Except I was assured that all would be taken care of. And I'm new here and everything, so what was I to do?"

"We'll get back to you. Don't leave town."

———

"OK, so you have in front of you the names of every child who is listed as attending the Easter egg hunt. And we need you to tell us everything you can remember regarding the activity of each of those kids during the hunt."

"I already told you, Officers, I don't really know the names and all ..."

"Let's start with a young man named Billy. That would be the one it seems started the kicking."

———

"This is the worst kind of case, Chief. Dead nursery school girl. Found facedown with the sharp end of a pair of school scissors, the kind we found all over the school art room, stuck right through her heart. Now she could have fallen on them by accident, I suppose. But how in the world?"

"Accident? I don't know. Has it ever happened in any grade, in any school?"

"We looked it up. Stabbings in bad districts over the years. Never with scissors, never by accident, that we found."

"Suicide? Not likely. And as La Chase said, kids will be kids, but this is … I just don't know."

"Here's the thing: No prints or DNA on the scissors. But somebody had to have touched them. The girl, the stabber, the somebody. So that somebody went to the effort to get rid of any sign. Gloves would do it."

"And remember, she was wearing white gloves to the hunt. As were most of the other little girls."

"Any mention of white glove residue on the scissors in the report?"

"Yeah, hers. But then they could very well have been her scissors."

"So stands to reason she would have held them at some point … They did find that speck of lipstick on one of her gloves. But then none of the nursery girls I questioned was wearing lipstick … heh, heh. DNA didn't match any of the teachers at the school, the ones who were across the street the whole time. Who knows?"

"And none of the staff was near enough to hear what must have been a noisy brawl?"

"They said they had a last-minute staff meeting, at a room across the street, because of some emergency that came up."

"Right. So let's start our inquiries with Billy and his parents."

———

"I don't understand, Officers," the father complained. "We've already talked with the police. You can't suspect Billy."

"We don't suspect anybody of anything. We're simply the detectives assigned to this investigation, and as such, it's necessary to ask a few questions. If some of the questions are ones you've already answered, we apologize. We're just trying to do our job."

"Yes, of course you are. Now honey, let's let the detectives do their thing. Get this over with," Billy's mom said.

"You're right, it's only that—"

"I know, I know."

"So could you please bring Billy in here?"

"I don't know, our lawyer said that we shouldn't."

"If you want to bring in a lawyer, that's your right, of course. But we only have a few straightforward questions."

"OK, that's fine. I'll get him."

"And you can be here, of course. But we must ask you to stay in the background."

———

"Billy, this won't take long. Just a few easy questions. We understand you were mad because you couldn't find an Easter egg, and that you went up to somebody in your class and you—what did you do, Billy?"

"I didn't do anything. I mean, I went right up to this mean girl, and I just looked at her and, well, you know."

"No, we don't really know, Billy. Please tell us. And why do you say that she was mean?"

"She just was. And she found this Easter egg. And you know something? I saw she had two, yeah two. I only asked her for one, because you see, I didn't have any. And she just …"

"What did she do, Billy? And what did you do?"

"I didn't do anything."

"What did you say to her? What happened?"

"You know what I said? I said she was a meany. That's what I said, 'you're a meany.' And then she laughed. Yeah that's what she did. And so I went and, and I just did it, real hard, too, because that's what she said."

"Did you see any other teacher with Mr. La Chase, Billy?"

"Uh, no. I don't think so."

"Are you sure?"

"I don't know. Can't remember."

"Fine, Billy, you're doing a great job. Can you show us exactly what you did? Show us how you kicked her, if that's what you did."

"Officers, I think that's enough. I really believe we should have a lawyer involved."

"That's certainly your right, sir. And we understand perfectly."

"He may have kicked her a good one, but I can't imagine he killed her. She certainly wasn't kicked to death."

"I know, and he just doesn't seem like, you know, your usual nursery school killer."

"No, he doesn't. And that leaves us with seventeen other young suspects and one, 'I'm new here, don't blame me,' teacher."

"One down, sixteen to go."

"I can't remember when I've had as much fun interviewing seventeen nursery school kids in a murder investigation. In fact, I can't remember ever interviewing any others, for any reason."

"How about the 'male or maybe female invisible teacher'? The one Billy can't seem to remember."

"And none of the little cuties remembers, for sure, seeing any other teacher in that room other than our very own Mr. La Chase. A few said 'maybe.' Or 'it's sort of possible.' Nobody seems to really know, one way or the other. Certainly nobody could serve as a court witness in La Chase's defense. But they all remember being hit, or kicked, or scratched by some classmate."

"And returning the favor."

"And most of the girls wore white gloves. But only her gloves seem to have touched the scissors in question."

"Quite a scene. You've got to feel a little sorry for La Chase. Unless he's the murderer, that is."

"You think?"

"I have no idea. I wish I knew."

———

"We found something."

"I'll take anything."

"Our email to the staff finally got a response from a teacher who came back to the school early: older female, stomach upset we're told, laid down in the principal's office and may have heard, or seen, something."

———

"Now, Ms. Williams, you said you came back from the meeting early."

"Yes, I stayed as long as I could. After forty-five years as an educator, those meetings don't get any better. The issue here was about teacher rivalry. It's never-ending. Plus my stomach was really, really upset. I left abruptly. And then went right to the bathroom, because I was—well you understand."

"We do. And we want to thank you for coming forth and talking with us."

"Isn't it just terrible? That poor little girl, and the school simply doesn't deserve—"

"Of course, and if you can just tell us what you saw and heard."

"Right, so I went into the principal's office to rest for a spell. It was locked, but I do have a key. And I lay down on the couch. Closed my eyes. You see, his office is right next to the gym, where the Easter egg hunt was held. And I heard this awful ruckus. More than you would normally expect at an activity of that sort. It's a playtime activity, for sure. But this was more than I would have ever allowed. Certainly not, not on my watch. And I've been at this for a number of years, young man."

"Did you observe anything that might be of interest?"

"I did find the strength to get up and open the side door just a crack, the one that opens onto the gym. And I saw, oh my, what I saw. It was something else. But then I felt myself getting sick again and I had to rush to the bathroom. You see, my insides were … well, not good."

"We understand. What did you see, however briefly?"

"I got a glimpse at a young man who I took to be Mr. La Chase. He's the new teacher here who was assigned to run the Easter egg hunt while the rest of us attended the interminable emergency meeting. He volunteered. And we're so shorthanded here just now and it seemed the only way."

"Of course. So you took this man to be La Chase. Are you sure it was La Chase?"

"That's what's so strange. Because initially, I naturally took this person to be our new teacher. But then I was really quite sick, and I had this funny feeling I was looking at a woman. And then I thought, well, this is crazy. And when I looked again I thought no, it has to be Mr. La Chase. I mean, who else? Can you answer me that?"

"Can you tell us what you remember about what you saw that made you think it could have been a woman?"

"Well, I must have been hallucinating."

"This is very important in this investigation. Please tell us what you remember."

"The person looked like Mr. La Chase. Except that, at first I thought I saw lipstick. You see, that's what drew my attention. The lipstick. But then I can't be sure of anything."

"And what happened then?"

"Well, I felt sick again, thought I was seeing things, and closed the door and went to the WC."

"And after?"

"I went right home. I felt terrible. And I figured it would all be taken care of. It always is. Kids will be kids."

———

"Where did she come from? To barge in on the Easter egg hunt just when all hell was breaking loose. Did she think she could fix everything? And what happened to that little girl? So did she agree with Billy? And also think the little girl was a meany? Had two Easter eggs. She thinks she can fix things. But actually, she ruins stuff every time. And I'm left holding the bag. I try. Try as hard as I can to do the right thing. Treat people the right way. But then things always seem to go … oh, I don't know, off into never-never land, I guess."

———

"He's such a bumbler. Doesn't he realize he needs my help, for God's sake? He gets himself into the most impossible situations. And I'm the only one who can get him out. Granted, this situation didn't turn out quite the way it should have, but then that little girl was certainly a meany. Actually, she was quite the bitch. Just like Billy said. I know that shouldn't have meant she had to die. But then things got out of control. Anyway, why in the world did she have those scissors in her pocket in the first place? No reason. No reason at all. Worse yet, she took them out when Billy kicked her the second time. And then, the goddamn fool, she swung them at Billy, hard, real hard. And La Chase saw it too. But, as usual, he just stood there, like a goddamn fool. So I reached for the scissors. She was swinging so hard, too hard, so I turned them away, away from Billy. And I didn't mean to turn them toward her, but there you have it."

"And to think I almost forgot to wipe off my lipstick. That would have messed things up."

———

"I'm your CEO, not your babysitter, for God's sake. But it looks like this board of directors of our revered Bright Sunshine Residence needs just that. One of you has informed me that La Chase is missing yet again. I've called this emergency board meeting for some answers. What are you doing to find him? What will you do to see to it this never happens again? We all know La Chase is a smart and dangerous schizoid. At least two personalities we know of. How about the time he got a job in a nursery school. We were damn lucky to get out of that one. But who knows what other mess he might get himself into?"

CHAPTER 18

NOTE ON A WINDSHIELD

The note he found on his windshield read, "I know your dirty little secret, but it's safe with me." Ernest had no doubts: *Clarke thinks he's so funny. Who else would leave such a stupid note on my car?*

The two had been best buddies ever since high school, a good twenty years ago. Went to separate colleges but stayed in touch. And now worked in the same up-and-coming Midwest city.

An unusual friendship, for sure. Ernest was a successful, albeit behind the scenes, do-the-research kind of lawyer. Always the nerdy kid. Retained the same profile as a young man. Clarke, on the other hand, had been a strapping, handsome, high school jock and college football scholarship winner. His scholarship was revoked in his second year, for reasons that never really came to light. Rumors of drugs and possible underage rape, just rumors though. Anyway, that was way back then. Presently, Clarke was … what exactly was Clarke now? An entrepreneur? A jack of all trades? A bartender? An almost-writer? A still-trying-to-find-himself kind of college grad? If indeed he did graduate. Bit of a mystery, not that it really mattered to Ernest.

The fact of the matter was that Clarke was fun to be around, in Ernest's estimation. If he didn't drink too much, which he did on occasion. They certainly made for an interesting pair during their regular outings.

Ernest remained reclusive, gawky, but in good shape. Whereas Clarke, fun-loving, ex-jock Clarke, was showing signs of going to seed.

Alice, Ernest's anorexic professor wife, displayed the parchment face similar to one of her many intellectual papers, papers that seemed to take up so much of her time that little was left to foster their marriage. She did find time for Clarke's wife, however, and they remained close. That would be the hardworking, overwhelmed with life's chores, zaftig, former cheerleader, Clementine. The woman who was pretty much singlehandedly raising two kids: William, age ten, plus an adopted son, Albert, age eleven. Both of whom Alice babysat on a regular basis. Alice's only close family tie had been a sister, one who had disappeared: left town some time ago, under mysterious circumstances.

Alice and Ernest stopped trying for kids of their own several years ago because of a medical condition the doctors couldn't seem to solve. Of course, Clarke was always guy-talk teasing Ernest about "shooting blanks" and "duds with empty balls." The irony here was that Alice and Ernest, both with successful careers, could well afford to have children, whereas Clementine was overwhelmed and underfunded. Always busy at home with the kids and housework. Clarke was forever off trying to find himself to be of much help.

—————

"Very funny, Clarke," Ernest said to start his phone call. "Just what sort of secret of mine are you going to keep?"

"What secret are you taking about, my man?"

"The one you referred to in the note you left on my car windshield."

"I don't know anything about any note on your windshield. Just tell me what kind of secret you have so I can hold it against you. Better yet, blackmail you with. Are you playing around with young boys? That's the little secret, isn't it?"

"Don't be ridiculous. And you're not funny. So, are you saying you did not leave a note on my windshield this morning?"

"What did I just tell you? Now tell me about those young boys."

"Stop kidding around. This is no joke. I mean, do you have any idea who would leave an off-the-wall note like that? You're the only one I know stupid enough to."

"Hey, cut out the personal stuff, you horse pucky. And stop accusing me."

"OK, we haven't had a night out for a while." said Ernest. "What about tonight? Boys' night out. Or are you too busy with important, high finance business matters?"

"Very fucking funny. Actually, I do have a shift at the bar tonight. But Bill owes me one, so I'm pretty sure I can work it out. Seven tonight, usual place?"

"You're on."

———

"OK, show me the note," Clarke said after they had ordered beers and bar snacks, seated at their regular table. "You brought it with you, I assume?"

"Yeah, of course I did."

Ernest pulled a folded piece of paper from his pocket. Opened it up revealing a piece of Super 8 Motel stationery with the "dirty little secret" note.

"It's typed with an old-fashioned typewriter. So I can't match your handwriting. Do you own a typewriter?"

"Cut the shit. You know I use a PC. The one that doesn't seem to be able to produce a novel. Or even a decent short story. So stop accusing me."

"Then the whole thing is somebody's idea of a joke. OK, let's forget about it. But you know it's going to bug me. Who in the world?"

So they forgot about it. Made it an early night out. Promised to stay in touch, as always, and went about their business.

A week later it happened again. Same message, same Super 8 Motel stationery.

"Clarke, you sure it's not you?" Ernest said into the phone. "Because if it is, that's OK. Just tell me the truth. We'll both have had a good laugh and be done with it. But I've got to tell you, it's driving me crazy. Is that what you want?"

"I don't want anything."

"OK. Tonight, the usual, if you're free? You're the only person I can imagine talking about this with. Haven't told the wife. No need to involve her."

———

"Here's the thing," Ernest started off the conversation that night, at their usual table. "I can't think of any bad secret. Nothing that might come up and cause something like this. So just what does this mystery person want from me?"

"Come on, now. I don't know what this person's story is, but you've got to admit, we all have secrets of one kind or another. I know I do. That's the way it goes."

"Fine. I'm not interested in your secrets. And I don't have any worth mentioning."

"Liar."

"I'm not a fucking liar. What's your point?"

"No point. No point at all. It's only that if you do have some kind of secret, something that's been in the back of your mind for a while, well, that might help you figure out just who this note writer is. And that's what you want, isn't it? It's driving you crazy, right? You really want to know who. Don't you?"

"Well, wouldn't you? What the hell does he want? He's crazy. Or she. Whatever. Crazy for sure."

"OK, here's the situation. You called me because you want a sounding board. Right?"

"I guess."

"So, we both know little bits and pieces about each other's background. And if you really want me to sort it out with you, here goes."

"Here goes what?"

"Well, what about Sally? What's the full story behind Sally?"

"Sally? Sally who?"

"Sally! The Sally you dated for a while and then she was found dead in a hotel room in Florida. Alongside her dead boyfriend. That Sally."

"If you're talking about Sally Lockhart, I have no idea what the dickens really happened to her or her murdered boyfriend. How would I know anything after all these years?"

"Sally Lockhart! I had forgotten her last name. But you didn't. You knew it right away."

"So?" said Ernest. "So what?"

"So, what happened to her?"

"You know very well what happened. Died of an overdose in a Florida hotel."

"Yes, and the boyfriend beaten to death in the same room," said Clarke.

"Stabbed and beaten," said Ernest. "And what does that have to do with me?"

"Stabbed? I thought the paper just said beaten. Anyway, I read something along the lines of you being in Florida at about the same time. If I'm not mistaken."

"You're mistaken. Well OK, yes, I was there, briefly. Didn't see Sally though. Had an argument with Alice and just took off for Florida. Told all this stuff to the police. And I was cleared of anything. Old hat. What's your point?"

"My point is, did you get away with murder?"

"Don't be stupid. And if you want to dig up old secrets: How about the one concerning why, exactly, you lost your scholarship?"

"That's a good one, my friend. But then nobody left me a threatening note."

"That wasn't a threatening note I got."

"Well, close enough. And I suspect the next one will be just that."

"Yeah, and how do you know there will be a next one? You're the sender, aren't you?"

"Shut up. I'm not your man."

"Well, you could have fooled me."

———

It came one week later, under the windshield wipers on the passenger's side, so you didn't notice it right away. But if you had a passenger, that person would probably spot the note first. So Ernest was making a point not to drive anybody anywhere these days.

This guy, girl, whoever, must work at a Super 8, or have stocked up on their stationery, thought Ernest as he eyed the latest missive. *This one was a picture. And that was all. Just a picture. A copy of an old, faded, black-and-white snapshot. A picture of a girl next to a guy. A palm tree in the background of a hotel lobby. It was hard to identify who they were. But of course he knew who they were. No doubt about it. Goddamn it to hell.*

———

"Sally with a guy, right?" said Clarke at their meeting place, as he looked at the snapshot Ernest handed over. "Where are they in the picture?"

"Who knows? And I'm not even sure if it's Sally."

"Sure it's Sally, who else?"

"OK, it's Sally, and this picture was taken in a Florida hotel. You can tell from the background. Art Deco stuff, and that's a palm tree in the lobby. Because, listen to me, I took the picture. So shut up and hear what I have to say. And if you repeat any of it, to anybody, I'll kill you. I mean it."

"Speak up, you little fucker. Not so quick this time to deny your 'dirty little secret'?"

"First of all, it was you, wasn't it? You put the note, I should say notes, on my windshield, didn't you?"

"You don't know that for sure."

"I know it, goddamn it. And if you don't own up, right here and now, that will be a second reason to kill you. And I'll do it. Believe me."

"OK, yes, it was me. It started as just a stupid little joke. Really. You know me."

"I do."

"But then, you responded … in such a funny way. After that, I just couldn't help myself. I did it again. And all that Super 8 stationery made it more like a detective story I might write."

"Write about something else, you little prick."

"Yeah, but you know something? I wasn't really thinking of Sally. At least not at first. I really wasn't. But then there was that picture. I've had it for years. In an old shoe box stuffed with all kinds of shit from my school days. Awards, a pile of sports sweater letters that never got sewn on, stuff like that. Plus pictures, a bunch. So it might sound weird, but every once in a while I would take out the box and look through it. Remembering the good old days, the ones I fucked up, I guess. But also to get ideas for stories I'm trying to write. For all the good it does me. Anyway, I'm just telling you that I've seen that picture over and over again. Never knew who it was for sure. Or where it came from. And maybe, in the back of my mind, I thought it might be Sally. But I really didn't know. Or how I got it. But … I knew right away who it was when I saw your reaction. So, what's the deal? What did you do, Mr. Bad Guy? By the way, do they have the chair as an option in this state?"

"You shut up and I'll tell you what happened. But if it gets out, you'll wish for the chair yourself."

"I believe you."

"Believe it. So first of all, let's get this straight: I'm not a bad guy. I think I would be called a victim of circumstances. But that's not how some might see it. And I could easily get screwed. Big time. Because, well … just because. So I'll tell you what the deal is. And I'm not really sure why I'm telling you all this. Except that I've been carrying this thing inside me for years. I feel like I'm going to explode. Maybe telling you will help. I hope so."

"Speak up, my man. Sounds like a great story for me to write."

"Reason number three to kill you."

"Just kidding."

"OK, here goes … I did go to Florida with Sally. Well, actually I followed her. And yes, I was dating Alice at the same time. But you see, here's the thing: Sally was pregnant. Or at least that's what she said. So I had two girlfriends. One very smart lady, on her way to becoming a college professor. And the other, a very sexy lady, on her way to marrying an unsexy man on his way to becoming a lawyer. I was smitten. In love big time. What she saw in me I couldn't say. Money, stability, I suppose. I didn't care. She was unbelievable, as I'm sure you remember."

"Yeah, she was."

"So anyway, when the pregnant thing reared its ugly head, I followed her suggestions to the letter. Florida, marriage, honeymoon. The plan was for us to come back as the happy newlyweds. Her plan. But I had an important exam coming up, so she went down first, registered in a hotel, in her name, with my cash. She was going to set the whole thing up a week in advance. But I went down a week early. Turns out my grades were good enough to skip the exam. And then, on a whim, mind you, before I surprised her in Florida by being early, I called up her doctor back home. Made up a story about being engaged, flying to Florida, nervous about her being pregnant. 'Would it be safe?' Seems she had seen him recently. He said it wasn't exactly kosher of him to say anything, but he did let it slip that she wasn't pregnant, never was as far as he knew.

"So she had lied to me, and I wanted to forget the whole thing and go home. But I was in love. I stayed. I placed a few more calls. And made a number of other disturbing discoveries. She claimed she was a history major, but there was no record of her being enrolled at school, no record of her working where she claimed she was employed. And my credit card showed a large withdrawal, in my name, without my knowledge, made the day before she left for Florida. I had my card, I assumed she'd snitched it, used it, and returned it. I was at a loss. Mad as hell. And falling out of love. But sort of still in love. If that makes any sense."

"It does."

"So, not knowing what to do, I went to the hotel where she said she was staying, sat in a far corner of the lobby reading the newspaper. I just sat there like that, waiting, not sure what to expect. It seemed like it at the time, but maybe not such a good idea after all. Anyway, she was driving me crazy. Have you ever felt that way about a girl?"

"Sure. Haven't we all, at one time or another?"

"Right. And so that was me. And guess what? She shows up after a while, with some guy. They get off the elevator and head out in a big hurry. Both drunk, or high, who knows? I couldn't believe it. I suppose I should have expected something like that. But my whole world was topsy-turvy."

"I guess."

"Seems the good part was, just like that, I wasn't in love anymore. It's unbelievable, how you can be so, so madly, head over heels in love one minute and then, because of whatever, it's all over. As though it never happened. In any event, I figured the best thing I could do was to follow them."

"They didn't spot you?"

"No. It was easy. They were out of it. Had no idea of what was going on around them. So first they drag themselves into a Chinese restaurant across the street. Come out about ten minutes later with a load of Chinese take-out bags. Then they head for the parking lot and get into a beat-up VW van. A few minutes later they're back at the hotel, carrying those greasy bags, bags all over the place. Both of them, arms are full. And they look like they're having a great time. Their only problem was standing up. They took a couple of stumbles before reaching the hotel elevator. But not before I got a few pictures of them."

"One of which," spoke up Clarke, "I've had in a shoe box for a while."

"That's right. Who knows how one of those ended up with you. Doesn't matter. Anyway, I followed them up to the room, close enough to get the number and then I returned to the lobby, having no clear idea of what to do next."

"What were you thinking? Did you want to get him? And what would you do with him if you did?"

"Just listen. I called the room on the hotel phone in the lobby." 'Hello?' I said. 'This is the hotel front desk calling. You seemed to have dropped a small paper bag in the lobby. Would you like a bellhop to bring it up to your room, sir?'

"There was a long pause at the other end of the phone. 'Are you sure?' he says in this slurred voice. 'I mean, what's in the bag? No, no, don't bother looking in the bag. Yeah, I guess you should bring the bag up here. Yes, here. And don't bother looking in the bag, not necessary. Good boy.'

"So I went up to the room, knocked. 'Room service, sir,' I said. 'I have your package here. The one I called up about.'

"First I heard some shuffling. Then the door opened a crack, but the door chain stayed in place.

"He says, 'You have a package for me?'"

"'Yeah,' I say, 'but you'll have to undo that chain for a second in order for me to hand it to you.'

"'What for?' he asks. 'Why can't you just … OK, here you go.'

"He undid the chain with some difficulty and reached his hand out.

"'Just give me the fucking package and get the fuck out of here.'

"And listen up, you should have seen what happened next. I'm a wimp. You know that. But something came over me. Like some super adrenaline power burst inside me and I was like, oh I don't know, 007. I kicked open the door and barged in. He stumbled backward and fell flat on his stupid drunken ass. And there I was: I looked around and saw her lying on the bed. Covered with a sheet. Passed out,

I assumed. Then I checked her out. And I couldn't believe it, but she didn't seem to be breathing. I checked again. No! Not breathing. Well, I did the breathing thing. The chest thing. Nothing. Dead. Dead. Dead. Overdose, I guessed. What next? My first thought was 911, so I headed for the phone. And then, out of the blue, the guy appears—the guy I last saw on the floor. And he pipes up with, 'What the fuck you doing?'"

"'I'm calling 911,' I said as I grabbed the phone.

"'I don't think so,' he growled while snatching the phone. 'We don't need any cops here, so you just get your ass out. And stay out. And don't say anything to anybody, you got that?'"

"I don't remember what I said. I do remember I was scared. Real scared. But adrenaline, or something, kicked in again and I grabbed him and he did the same to me and before you knew it, we were slamming each other around. I mean really hard."

"Well," said Clarke, "that's not the Ernest I know."

"You're right. And this guy was certainly bigger than scrawny me, but he was really high on something. So I must have had the advantage, even though I'm certainly not the fighter type. Anyway, he was pounding me but also pounding on the walls, the floor, everywhere. His blows were crazy. His hands and arms were all over the place. Like he didn't know what he was doing. But it did hurt, the few times he connected with me. And I remember just looking around, and then I grabbed a Chinese shish kebab spike that was sticking out of one of the bags. Small but sharp. I stabbed him with it. And something happened to me. Because I just kept stabbing, and stabbing. Then I found another spike and stabbed some more."

"I don't believe this."

"Believe it … I finally stopped. There was blood all over the place. And I was in a room with two bodies. This guy and my former girlfriend. I forgot all about 911 and only thought about myself. And how to get out of this mess. My first thought was, what to do about the blood? The stuff that covered me. So I took off all my clothes and got into the shower and stayed there for a long time. Long enough to wash off every bit of the red I could see. I got out and found a small suitcase of hers and stuffed all my clothes inside. And then dressed myself in his clothes, some clean ones I found laying around. A little large, but not bad. Afterward I went around the room with a towel and wiped off every surface I could find. Hey, I've seen *CSI.* Then I left. Without a trace of me ever being there."

———

"And you're here for a book reading, Mr. Samuel?"

"Please, just call me Clarke."

"Fine, well, we're very happy to provide you with space in our bookstore. And I've heard very good things about your novel. But I must confess I haven't had time to read it yet. Can you tell me a bit about it?"

"Sure. Briefly, it's about a guy who kills his girlfriend's lover with a Chinese shish kebab spike, and gets away with it."

"That's it? The guy gets away with murder?"

"Well, for a while. And then something happens."

"What's that?"

"You see, his close friend writes a novel about it. With fictional characters and name changes. But …"

"But what?"

"Well, a detective who was around when the murder happens gets an advance copy of the novel, puts two and two together and nabs the guy."

"So what happens then?"

"You'll have to read my novel. And I've got a new novel in the works, if you're interested, about a high school jock who loses it all because of a drug-related rape charge that results in a birth. The child is adopted by the jock/rapist and his wife. Oh, by the way, the woman who was raped happens to be the sister of the wife of the killer in my current book, my first novel. The rapist rises from the ashes to become a famous author. It's kind of complicated. You'll have to read my second novel, when I'm finished."

BEHIND THE SCENES

EDITOR   Susan T. Landry is a freelance editor with
a long career as both a medical manuscripts
editor and creative copy editor. She is also
a writer and has recently published her first
book. susanlandry@gmail.com